DECEPTION

Lexi Brooke's acting skills were stretched to the limit when she accepted the job of Personal Assistant to charismatic Cade Chamberlayne, head of the family-owned cosmetics and jewellery empire, Cosmogems. On a business trip to California, Cade discovered Lexi was not what she appeared to be, and in her efforts to convince him of the truth, she was to have a far more turbulent time than she had bargained for.

JOYCE JOHNSON

DECEPTION

Complete and Unabridged

LINFORD
Leicester

First published in Great Britain in 1993

First Linford Edition
published 2006

British Library CIP Data

Johnson, Joyce
    Deception.—Large print ed.—
    Linford romance library
    1. Love stories
    2. Large type books
    I. Title
    823.9′14 [F]

    ISBN 1–84617–218–7

Published by
F. A. Thorpe (Publishing)
Anstey, Leicestershire
Set by Words & Graphics Ltd.
Anstey, Leicestershire
Printed and bound in Great Britain by
T. J. International Ltd., Padstow, Cornwall

This book is printed on acid-free paper

1

Out of the corner of her eye, Lexi
Brooke noticed the two youngsters
following her. They'd been hanging
around the entrance when she'd turned
into the underground station. Part of
her survival kit over the past ten years
had been a sensitive antennae to
trouble and she felt its familiar
vibrations now. Instinctively she kept
her head down, concentrating on
maintaining the short, precise steps
she'd been practising. If she'd guessed
correctly, the two boys were fooled by
her rather dowdy appearance, a complete contrast to her normal self.

Morning rush hour was over, the
crowds had thinned, and as she went
to the ticket machine, Lexi was able to
keep a wary eye on her followers. As
she began to reach into a plain, old
fashioned handbag for her ticket

money, the youths moved closely in on each side of her, one jostling her sharply from the left, the other making a snatch at her handbag from the right. Her reflex action was swift and automatic. In a graceful upward twist she spun round to grasp each one by the arm, jerking them together so they were caught off balance. There was a sharp crack as their heads met.

'Ouch — sorry about that,' she murmured, as they reeled back. Looking round the station concourse for help, her hands noted sadly how thin and bony the young arms were. She called out, 'Can someone help me?'

If current stories were to be believed, people should hurry by, eyes averted, terrified of being involved. But Lexi was an optimist, and always expected the best from people. Besides there was something about her — even dressed as she was today. At drama college, they'd called it 'stage presence'. It worked now.

Several people stopped, gaping in

amazement. A young girl gathered up the contents of her bag which had fallen to the ground, and two large men who looked like useful rugby players relieved her of the boys.

'What shall we do with them?' one asked, giving his captive a shake.

'Don't hurt them.' Lexi straightened her jacket. 'They're only schoolkids — truanting, I suppose.' The boys looked scared, still dumb struck from their swift capture. She frowned at them severely. 'You picked the wrong person this time. Just because I'm female . . . I hope it'll teach you a lesson — things aren't always what they seem. How many times have you tried this?'

The taller of the two mumbled something incomprehensible, still very frightened. Her soft heart twisted in pity, but she maintained a stern school marm act. 'I should hand you over to the transport police. Fortunately for you, I'm in a hurry — but if I ever catch sight of you here again, I will turn you in. Do you understand?' At her nod the burly men reluctantly released their prisoners who instantly fled.

'That was impressive! You should have called the police though,' one of the men said, but both looked at her with frank curiosity.

Lexi shrugged. 'I'm not hurt and they didn't get my purse so there's no harm done. It's just sad, that's all.' She remembered her own rebellious school-days; she could well have ended up like that, hanging about, looking for apparently vulnerable victims.

'I'm already late for an appointment and I've probably missed my train. Thanks for your help.' She moved away, smiling, 'It confirms my faith in human nature.'

'A pleasure to help — and where did you learn to do that?' They were still eyeing her speculatively.

'Oh, here and there,' she answered vaguely. 'There are more dangerous places in the world than London's underground. Thanks again.' With a farewell wave she broke into her usual long-legged sprint in an effort to catch the train and make up for lost time.

It was true. She'd been in far more potentially dangerous situations and had often been grateful that she'd learned basic self defence before going to work in some of the less pleasant areas of South America. And, in the seedier districts of New York, she'd felt more secure knowing she could protect herself in case of attack.

The incident on the station had done nothing more than disturb her concentration, and she needed all her wits about her to get through the next few hours. She must have been mad to agree to her friend Anya's plan.

Relaxing into the swaying rhythm of the train, she closed her eyes, shrinking her body, dropping her shoulders to a slight aging roundness, slackening her facial muscles to disguise the youthful tautness of her skin. She was going to be late but there was nothing she could do about it, and fretting only made things worse. Lexi didn't believe in wasting unnecessary time and energy on 'what might have beens.'

★   ★   ★

She was disappointed in the unimpressive exterior of Chamberlayne Cosmogems Ltd. For a company whose main investment was in glamour, the outside of their building complex could have benefited from a face lift, Lexi thought, as she checked her watch, before going through the main entrance door. Only fifteen minutes late, not too bad. She breathed a sigh of relief which quickly changed to a startled exclamation of surprise. The interior was a totally different story.

Once through the main doorway, black glass doors led into a world where style and opulence were reflected everywhere, from the deep pile carpet underfoot, to the discreetly stated floral arrangements on marble plinths.

Two attractive, beautifully made-up, young women were on duty in a reception area. One smiled as Lexi went up to the desk.

'Lexi Brooke. I have an appointment for . . .'

'Oh, yes, they've been waiting for you,' the girl cut in, with more than a hint of disapproval.

'I'm sorry I'm late,' she apologised.

'You'd better go in straight away. The lifts are over there — top floor, Mrs Honeywell's office. I'll ring to say you're on your way. Oh — and best of luck,' she added, doubtfully, seeing the plainly dressed, colourless looking woman as an unlikely contender for the post of personal assistant to Cade Chamberlayne.

The mirrored walls of the lift told Lexi that her make-up was still discreetly effective, and her hair still restrained by its unbecoming style. Large tinted glasses hid most of her face in any case! Confidence reassured, she stepped out into the corridor.

7

The suite of offices on the top floor was furnished to the same luxurious standards as the ground floor. To the right was an open plan office crammed with all the latest technology, and Lexi sensed a frenzied work pace. On the left were several panelled doors; one marked 'Madeleine Honeywell, Secretary,' was partially open.

As she knocked, an attractive and elegantly groomed maturer version of the downstairs receptionist came to greet her. 'You must be Lexi Brooke. You're late. You were first on the list, but we've started interviewing to save time. There're only three applicants shortlisted.'

'I'm sorry I'm late,' Lexi said again, 'but it was unavoidable.'

'If you'd wait in there, Mr James will call you when they're ready.' With a cool nod she indicated a reception area with plenty of comfortable leather armchairs outside her office, and Lexi walked over to the far end of the room, remembering to shorten her stride, feeling Mrs Honeywell's eyes on her back.

The walls were covered in photographs of beautiful women displaying exquisitely designed jewellery. The Chamberlayne hallmark seemed to be feminine loveliness enhanced to perfection by the art of Cosmogems. So far, she'd seen no-one who wasn't up to that standard. Except herself! Even her fellow applicant for the job had a model figure and features to match, and obviously hadn't believed the advert which had so intrigued both herself and Anya!

A door near the secretary's office opened, and a tall fair man ushered out a young woman. 'You can either wait, or come back in an hour. We should know by then.' Friendly blue eyes smiled in a tanned handsome face. 'Miss Brooke?' he asked, enquiringly.

So — she was second. Lexi took a deep breath and walked carefully forwards.

'I'm James Chamberlayne.' He held

the door open for her, standing back as she went into a large, thick carpeted room. The far wall was glass from top to bottom, with cream linen blinds drawn well back. Behind the desk by the window was a swivel chair. The room appeared to be empty, and Lexi looked round her uncertainly.

'Over there, by the desk. Sit down, Miss Brooke.' The voice from behind was clear, but deep, and carried a commanding authority. It was not a voice to ignore, and Lexi went to sit in a smaller chair facing both the full glare of light from the huge window, and the imposing swivel.

The owner of the voice came round to the front of her, holding out his hand, and Lexi stood up to take it. The pressure was firm, but brief. She imagined a slight tingle from the warmth, and looked up into eyes which first she saw as green, then noticed were unusually flecked with topaz.

There was no smile in his keen appraisal. 'Mr James Chamberlayne,' he nodded towards the fair haired man who had seen Lexi into the room and was now sitting in the large chair. 'He'll conduct the first part of the interview. I'm Cade Chamberlayne,' he added.

For Lexi, the introduction was unnecessary. She'd researched both the company and its managing director before deciding to apply for the job. The unusual advertisement had initially caught her attention, and the company name was familiar, but she hadn't bargained for its prestigious position in the stock market league table. During the last five years, Chamberlayne Cosmogems had soared to prominence, mainly through the efforts of dynamic young Cade Chamberlayne, who had taken over from his grandfather. She'd seen lots of pictures of Cade in the press and in the company's literature. He was always accompanied by stunning women, whose glamour was a suitable setting for the famous Chamberlayne jewellery. This year he'd been nominated for the Royal Award of

Young Businessman of the Year. She had been intrigued and impressed by the track record of both man and company, and felt that a spell working for them would help her on the career path she'd planned. She also knew that James and Cade were cousins.

Cade Chamberlayne returned to the chair in the corner of the room, from which he could study Lexi in profile as she dealt with the questions. James, head down, was scanning her c.v. Conscious of Cade's scrutiny, she gave him a covert look. In the flesh, he was even more charismatic than on the pages of the glossy brochures she'd studied, along with the Company's annual balance sheet. He wasn't handsome in the conventional sense, as James was. The planes of his face were a little too angular, although the full mouth was well shaped. His thick, dark hair was carefully cut to fit the well groomed business image. He was tall, and he'd moved back to his chair with the lithe graceful movement of an athlete. Cool and aloof, Lexi guessed; a very different character from his cousin, James, who was all charming friendliness as he asked the conventional questions about her qualifications and skills — all of which were meticulously set out in her c.v.

'Distinction in your college business diploma — a prize for computing. Very impressive, Miss Brooke. I see you've only just finished your course though — a little later than most students. There's a very long gap between leaving school and starting college.'

Lexi opened her mouth to reply, but Cade Chamberlayne had moved silently across the room. 'If you don't mind, James, I'll take over. You've established that Miss Brooke has all the correct qualifications for the position.' He looked at her comprehensively, eyes sweeping over her from head to foot, lingering on her beautiful legs. Long and shapely, it had been impossible to disguise them, even with thick tights and flattish shoes. She resisted the

13

temptation to pull down the beige skirt of her plain suit, and crossed her ankles instead — she hoped, primly.

Cade leaned back, swivelling very slightly in the chair. He ignored the c.v. in front of him. 'You've had a variety of jobs in the last ten years. Flying nanny, chauffeuse, cook, market research, travel courier. Quite a mixed bag. Aren't you going to find business dull in comparison?' He frowned at her, and Lexi was thankful she hadn't included her brief acting and modelling career, and also her more zany short-term jobs, such as a Las Vegas croupier! She knew, looking as she did now, it would be difficult to believe she'd once played hostess in a very expensive and exclusive restaurant in Beverly Hills. And that was when she'd applied for a job in the kitchen!

She was ready for the question. It was an obvious one. 'No, not at all. It's because I've had a variety of jobs that I'm ready now for a solid career. And your products aren't dull, Mr

Chamberlayne. Skin care, cosmetics, and jewellery are glamorous.'

'You won't have a lot of contact with the products. It's the dull routine business I want my PA to deal with, so get rid of the notion that you'd be a part-time model.' He spoke almost angrily, and Lexi bit her lip.

'I don't want to be a model — my interest is in the business side of your organisation.' She spoke evenly. 'That's why I took a business course.'

'You've been a rolling stone for a long time.' He ignored her explanation, and Lexi was glad of the spectacles to hide the annoyance in her eyes. The job was well within her capabilities — she'd studied the comprehensive job specification thoroughly. Surely it was the present and future which mattered, but Cade Chamberlayne was insistent, leaning forward, green eyes fixed intently on her face. 'Perhaps you'd care to tell us why you seem to be unable to settle to any particular job or career for any substantial length of time?'

Lexi was puzzled. The man seemed hostile — if he disapproved of her past why had he shortlisted her? She imagined that there would be a lot of applicants, no doubt attracted by the glamorous image of Chamberlayne's, in spite of the downbeat advert! She pushed back her own outspoken persona. 'In for a penny, in for a pound' she remembered Anya's cliché that morning when she'd wished her good luck.

'Certainly, Mr Chamberlayne,' she answered briskly. 'I left school when I was sixteen. I had to earn a living. We . . . ' she hesitated, mentally asking forgiveness from her mother and father who'd begged her to stay on and go to college, ' . . . couldn't afford to carry on my education. I was — am — a very independent person. I didn't want to be a burden to my parents so I took the first job that came along. One job led to another, and I began to enjoy the variety. As you can see from my c.v. I've travelled a lot, worked abroad, done many things. I know now what I want to do, and what I don't want to do.' She paused, but Cade continued to stare silently at her, dark eyes, unfathomable, the merest hint of perplexity in their depths. 'I do want this job, Mr Chamberlayne. I know I can do it, and do it well. I feel it's time I settled down for a while.' She could have bitten her tongue on the last words.

Cade Chamberlayne pounced, as she knew he would. 'For a while?' He repeated her phrase. 'I don't see this job as a staging post between adventure bouts. From what you say, you'd be off in a few months, when you're trained, and we shall have to go through the whole process again. And you've no commercial experience,' he seemed delighted to add.

'I'm very well qualified — and I'm adaptable, a quick learner. I've had to be — that's the advantage of varied experiences.'

'It's important to have a committed, stable person as my personal assistant.'

He growled at her, tapping her c.v. 'This record doesn't show stability, and you don't seem committed to anything.'

Lexi took a deep breath. This man was challenging her — and she could never resist a challenge. She played the card she banked on getting her the job. 'Mr Chamberlayne, in all fairness, do I look an unstable adventuress, only interested in modelling? From your ad — what was it — 'Plain and Sensible — glamour a disadvantage'? I'd say I'm exactly the sort of person you're looking for.'

Cade's eyes were alert, boring into her, assessing the plain but good suit and white linen shirt, pale brown hair, combed flatly behind the ears, prim expression. Lexi's heart pounded and as she held her breath his eyes travelled down her body again, but his expression was inscrutable. He seemed about to say something, but shrugged and stood up. 'We'll let you know. There's still another applicant to see. James, would you bring in the eleven thirty appointment?' He glowered down at Lexi as she gathered her bag and gloves. 'You were late, too,' he said accusingly. 'I can't stand unpunctuality — it's a sign of a disorganised mind. Not an asset for this position.'

'I . . . ' Lexi tried to explain.

'Never mind. I don't like excuses either.' He picked up a folder from the desk, went back to his chair in the corner, and ignored her completely.

She was severely tempted to tell him what he could do with his job. He was insufferably smug and pompous and she wondered if she really wanted to work for him. James Chamberlayne held open the door for her, looking apologetic. What a pity he didn't need a personal assistant! 'Thank you — both, for your time,' she said, resisting the urge to abandon her precise manner, and sweep out, head held up to her full height.

Mrs Honeywell was more friendly and smiled at her as she came out. 'I expect you're glad that's over.'

'Yes. Interviews can be stressful.' She didn't add, 'Particularly with someone like Cade Chamberlayne.'

Annoyed that he'd managed to get under the skin so much, she sat down to wait, leafing through the expensive glossies on the marble table. It was part of the company's stock in trade, to keep up with the fashion world and she became absorbed in the latest designs in Italian fashion jewellery.

The last applicant came out, looking very pleased with herself, smiling provocatively over her shoulder at James as he followed her out. He said to the three women, 'We shan't keep you long. If you'd like to wait, there's fresh coffee — help yourselves.' He lingered, as if reluctant to begin the conference with his cousin, but an impatient call from inside the room, pulled him back as though he was on a piece of elastic.

Lexi laughed. 'I'm sure he'd rather stay here and have coffee with us!'

Her two rivals looked astonished. 'I know where I'd rather be,' the younger and prettier girl said. 'In there with Mr Chamberlayne.'

The other nodded agreement. 'Absolutely. What a charmer!'

'James, you mean?' Lexi was puzzled.

'No, Cade, of course! He'd be a dream to work for.' The young girl sighed, 'But I don't suppose I stand a chance.'

Lexi shrugged. It sounded a very different interview from hers. 'Have some coffee,' she offered. 'I'll get it.'

A flask of fresh coffee stood on a hot plate between the two offices. She poured two cups and handed them to the others. As she lifted the flask to pour her own, the door handle of Cade's office turned. She paused, about to return to her seat, but froze as the voices inside reached her. They had stopped, just behind the door, as if to pick up the threads of an argument.

Cade's voice, impatient, was unmistakeable. 'I've told you, James, I don't want any more would-be models. Why do you think I've resisted having another personal assistant for so long? I've had enough of them. Why the other two applicants applied . . . ? Can't even read properly — plain, sensible, clever — that's what I need.'

'That's it then.' James' lower key reply was regretful. 'No contest. Let's get it over with.'

'Get rid of the other two and send her in,' Cade commanded as the door opened. Lexi moved quickly to get back to her seat.

James coughed and hesitated, before he spoke to the three women. 'Er . . . we've reached a decision. It's been very difficult, you're all very suitable . . . '

He doesn't like to upset people, Lexi thought. He's a ditherer — likes to be liked. She doubted whether his cousin Cade would have that problem!

He spoke in a rush, as if anxious to get an unpleasant task over. 'Miss Brooke, would you go back and see Mr Cade for a moment please.'

Lexi's stomach did a flip. Presumably

she'd got the job, and was pleased about that, but felt a strange reluctance to go back into the room with Cade Chamberlayne.

Re-entering the large office, she willed herself to appear calm and cool, maintaining the aura of plain and sensible efficiency which was the apparent key to success. But maybe she hadn't got the job. Perhaps this was a second interview — a one to one grilling without the diluting presence of James.

Cade Chamberlayne disabused her of that notion straight away. He unfolded his long length from the swivel chair and again held out his hand. 'Miss Brooke, I'm offering you the job.' The same brief but firm clasp. The same warmth ran from her fingers to her wrist. 'Now,' he flicked back a grey silk cuff to look at his watch. 'I've just time for a lightning tour, then I'll turn you over to Mrs Honeywell. She'll brief you on general routine. My personal work . . .' he made it sound quite threatening,

' . . . we'll attend to when I get back.'

'Get back?'

'From the States. My flight leaves in two hours. I can give you half an hour. Don't let's waste time.'

'But — I don't think, I'm not sure . . . ' Lexi panicked.

Frowning, he turned back. 'What?' He was terse. 'You do accept the job? You said you wanted it. Or are you one of those fools who wastes everyone's time going to interviews and then deciding it's not quite what you wanted?' He glared down at her, the full mouth compressed to a hard line.

Lexi could see no trace of the warmer topaz flecks. She swallowed. Cade's energy was pulsating. Now he was moving she could see the urgency of his movement. He'd been cooped up too long — now he wanted action. Impulsively, she responded. 'Yes, I'll take the job. Thank you.'

'Hmm.' A cross between a grunt and a snort was her only acknowledgement as he swept her out of the office towards the row of elevator doors. 'The top floor is the administration section. You've seen most of it.' They were in the lift, his tall body dominating the space. She kept well back. The fluorescent strip was tell-tale bright, and she didn't like the way Cade's eyes flicked searchingly over her face and figure.

* * *

The third and second floors housed the cosmetic and skin care laboratories, the first floor — the jewellery workshops and photographic studios. Everyone appeared absorbed and busy, seeming to know Cade who greeted many of them by name as he whisked her through the building, firing information as fast as he walked. With her assumed shortened stride, she found it hard to keep up.

He spoke rapidly, automatically, as if he'd said it many times before. 'Cosmogems was founded by my great grandfather, Jabez Chamberlayne, in eighteen-ninety — a tin miner who had to emigrate mid nineteenth century. He made some money in South Africa and Mexico, returned to England and, with my great grandmother, made and sold jewellery from a small house in Islington.'

Lexi shot him a sidelong glance. What a bald account. The full story was much more romantic than that! Obviously grandson Cade was a practical, down-to-earth fellow — a soul lacking imagination and romance.

He continued briskly, 'Although we're called Cosmogems, the cosmetic section was added later . . . '

'By your Great Aunt Elizabeth,' Lexi supplied, thinking it was time she got in on the act, 'who was a great gardener, specialising in herbal remedies, and who saw skin care potential in her plants. Cosmetics, the art of make-up, was developed by her daughter, your second cousin, Rowena. In nineteen-hundred-and-one, Chamberlayne Gems became Chamberlayne Cosmogems, moving from Islington to Kilburn. In nineteen-sixty your father moved out of the city and built this present factory and office complex. In nineteen-eighty-one, Chamberlayne Cosmogems was launched on to the stock market, family control being retained by buying the majority of the stock. You were appointed Managing Director five years ago with a ten per cent controlling interest.' She paused for breath, before concluding, 'Since the company's been under your direction, output and profits have soared, particularly export sales. The company shares are quoted at 542.30. Apart from a small downward turn last week, there's been little movement in the last six months.'

Cade's expression was shuttered, apart from the faintest movement in the neck pulse, at the end of her recital. 'You appear to have done a thorough research job on my company. Congratulations. Is there anything else you'd like to tell me?'

'Oh, yes. There's a plan to diversify

into publishing — starting with a very upmarket glossy. Your niece, Bella's idea — a magazine aimed at high profiling the company's cosmetics and jewellery. Personally, I don't think it's a good idea.' Her bubbling enthusiasm had led her into danger, and she hadn't noticed inscrutability give way to anger, as Cade thrust his hands into his pockets.

'You don't?'

'No, I'll tell you why . . . '

Cade cut in swiftly, voice cold. 'I think we can dispense with your opinion at this moment. Well informed though it may be, you can't possibly know all the implications. Darn it, you don't even work here yet! I'd prefer you to keep your theories to yourself until you have a thorough knowledge of Cosmogems.' He looked furious.

Lexi frowned, annoyed with herself. She'd forgotten Miss Plain and Sensible, and although she ached to challenge Cade Chamberlayne she knew she had to back track.

'I'm sorry,' she said quietly, but

couldn't help adding, 'perhaps you'd like to withdraw your offer of the job?'

'Don't tempt me,' he retorted, shooting another glance at his watch. 'I don't have time now for that luxury, and I rarely change my mind once I've reached a decision. If it's wrong, I deal with the consequences — later.'

The implication was clear. She would be very much on trial.

He didn't speak again until they were back on the top floor. There was no sign of James, or the other applicants. Mrs Honeywell was the only person in the management suite, and Cade went into her office. 'Madeleine, Miss Brooke starts work as my personal assistant on Monday. Can you handle it until I get back? I'll expect her to have a complete knowledge of our procedures by the end of the week. You can clear that room between James' and my office. That'll do for a start.'

'I'll see to it, Cade.' Mrs Honeywell gave him a warm, admiring look.

She obviously saw him as a wonder-man, Lexi thought in annoyance, but was disarmed by the older woman's friendliness when she spoke.

'I'm so glad you're joining us, Miss Brooke — Lexi? I'm Madeleine.' She held out her hand, then turned to her boss. 'I've checked your case — everything's fine. See you Friday. You'd better hurry or you'll miss the plane. Have a good time.'

Cade gave her a sardonic look. 'Thanks, but you know it won't be a picnic, especially in California. I'll be glad to get back.' He looked pointedly at Lexi. 'Until Friday then.' He patted Mrs Honeywell on the shoulder. 'Take care, Maddy.'

The smile from the topaz flecked eyes was warm and affectionate, and Lexi felt a pang at the marked contrast of his cool glance at her.

He left the office and Mrs Honeywell sighed. 'He works far too hard. He's under a lot of strain these days. I'm so glad we persuaded him to appoint a personal assistant again.'

'It's a new job then, not a replacement?'

'He used to have a PA, years ago, when he first took over — well a succession of them, but he preferred to work alone . . . just lately though . . . ' She broke off, and looked warily at Lexi.

'Yes?' Lexi was puzzled. She was certain that Madeleine Honeywell had been about to say something indiscreet.

'Nothing. Everything's fine — he's just very busy.' She finished quickly, flipping through papers on her desk. 'If you'll fill in these forms, sign your contract, you'll be on the pay roll from Monday.'

Lexi completed the formalities quickly, barely scanning the closely printed contract. A quick peek into her 'office', currently a windowless cupboard piled with storage boxes and files, decided her she'd had enough of Chamberlayne Cosmogems for one day.

2

On the way home she shopped extravagantly, buying sparkling wine, expensive French cheese, and some fresh salmon. Anya finished work early on Fridays and was already at her flat in Chiswick. She met Lexi at the door.

'And?' she asked, excitedly.

'I got it — whether I want it . . . ?'

'Come and tell me about it. It looks like celebration time.' She relieved Lexi of her parcels.

'I had to do something wild. I thought I'd go mad, keeping up that Miss Prim routine. I knew we were both in tonight, for a change, so I thought I'd cook us something.'

'Wonderful.' Anya's eyes lit up in anticipation. Lexi was a gourmet cook when she had the time and when the occasion warranted it.

'Pour me a glass of wine, Anya,

there's a love. I must get out of this — this drag act!'

Her friend laughed, and began to unpack the food. 'That's more like you,' she commented, as Lexi came back fifteen minutes later.

'Thank goodness! It feels more like me.' She'd changed her nondescript 'safe' beige suit for cerise pants and a black top. Contact lenses had replaced her thick, dark tinted glasses. Where Cade Chamberlayne's eyes were a subtle diffusion of green and topaz, hers were a deep grey with only a hint of green. She ran her fingers through the loosened curtains of newly washed thick, shiny hair, her face now cleansed of the deceiving make-up. With a grimace, she massaged her scalp, letting out an exhalation of relief as she reached for the wine Anya had poured.

'That's better.' Taking a long sip, she flopped down on to the sofa and looked over the rim of her glass. Her heart shaped face, with its full generous mouth and wide eyes, was serious.

'Anya, it's no good, I can't possibly go through with it. You'll have to phone on Monday. Say I've disappeared — had an accident! Anything! There's no way I can fool Cade Chamberlayne for more than a couple of hours!'

'You fooled him at the interview — you got the job!' Anya was triumphant, marvelling at the contrast between the colourless 'mouse' who'd left the flat that morning, and the glowingly attractive woman opposite.

Tall, slender and shapely, with a slim waist, there was a lithe grace of movement about Lexi which had once offered the chance of a modelling career. Her features were a shade irregular, but she had an elusive quality of attraction, a warmth of expression and a smile which made everyone want to smile back. But her spirit was too restless, her energy too exuberant, to maintain the discipline needed to be a top model.

'I could never feel it was real,' she'd confided to Anya. 'I want to live in the real world. There's so much out there.'

And that's what she'd done. Travelling the world, she'd taken on any job that turned up, sometimes working for third world charities, earning nothing but her keep. Sometimes, as in the Beverley Hills hostess job, earning enough to save towards her 'when I settle down' nest egg. The roving life had been so appealing that it was ten years before she felt a yearning for a permanent base — a home of her own. She began to envy Anya — a fellow rebel at school against authority, who had finally buckled down, gone to college, and was now a highly paid accountant for a multi-national company.

'It's so comfortable here,' Lexi sighed, snuggling deeper into the soft leather sofa. 'I love the way you've furnished it.'

'I suppose it's worth the hard work,' Anya replied, adding wistfully, 'but I haven't had the fun you've had. Tell me what happened this morning? What's the firm like — and Cade Chamberlayne?'

Lexi laughed, suspecting again that although their relationship was one of firm friendship, it was nourished by Anya's love of vicarious experiences. She told her first about the boys at the tube station.

Anya shook her head. 'I can't believe how plain you made yourself look — and so much older — it's unbelievable.'

'Not really. A touch of stage make-up, all part of my drama training. The hardest part was to act 'sensible.' The number of times I wanted to burst out and tell Cade Chamberlayne just what I thought of him . . . '

'But you are going to take the job. It's just the practical experience you need before you think of starting your own business.'

'I don't think I can keep up the 'plain and sensible' persona. Cade Chamberlayne is no fool. He's bound to see through me.'

'Rubbish. You're a great actress. Besides, think of the advantages — no more hassle from flirtatious bosses!'

Lexi giggled. 'That will be a relief. No more promotion offers, or plum acting parts dangled before me if only . . . ' She rolled her eyes suggestively in a meaningful wink.

'Don't — that's horrible,' Anya protested. 'I prefer the homely, sensible look.'

'But you've got a point — and you're right. It would be the perfect job — working closely with the head of a company like Cosmogems. I'd feel such a fraud though.'

'Nonsense — you're still you, you're not claiming any qualifications you don't have. You're just giving Cosmogems what they advertised for.'

'Well . . . '

'And didn't you say you've already signed a contract — no backing out now. You must give it a go — for a while.'

'That was a bit foolish,' she admitted,

37

little knowing just how much she would come to regret her impulse in the weeks to come. 'But there was something about Cade Chamberlayne, and Cosmogems. I was just swept along.' She stood up decisively. 'All right — you've persuaded me — I will take it. After all, what can he do to me?' Her breath caught in her throat, she paused fractionally, then pushed him and Cosmogems out of her mind. 'I'm now going to act the role of Master Chef and cook us the most amazing gourmet dinner. Let's have fun this week-end. I don't want to think about Monday morning.'

★ ★ ★

Lexi felt much less sanguine when Monday morning did arrive. She had to get up very early to apply the careful make-up which flattened the creamy tones of her skin, and narrowed the lines of her full mouth. A subtle touch was the fine highlighting of the lines from nose to mouth, brush strokes which aged her by five years at least. Shaded hollows under the cheek bones fined down her full heart-shaped face, enhancing the prim, compressed look she was aiming for. The deep honey gold of her hair had already been colour rinsed down to a nondescript pallor and pulled back into a coiled plait. The result satisfied her, prim and dignified looking, her age could have been anywhere between twenty-five and forty, although obviously her c.v. had had to show a truthful twenty-seven. A dark navy twin of the sensible beige interview suit completed the transformation. She nodded to the reflected image. 'Hi there, Hetty Smythe. I never thought you'd come in useful!'

Years ago, Lexi had played the part of a dedicated librarian in a murder mystery. It was a dreadful play, and fortunately Miss Smythe was murdered in Act One, but she remembered the prim, colourless little cameo part, and had modelled her new persona on

Hetty, taking care not to overstate the cliché. How she wished that all she had to do now was walk on stage, say her lines, and drop gracefully dead behind a sofa when the murderer shot her in the back! What she was doing now was for real and, for the umpteenth time, she regretted giving in to Anya's persuasions.

'Well,' she said defiantly to Hetty, 'here goes — it's all his fault for putting such a ridiculous advert in the paper.' She wished she'd never seen it — an impressive four column inch advert, setting out job description and qualifications needed for Cade Chamberlayne's personal assistant. It was very succinct and business-like, but it was the last line which particularly intrigued Lexi and Anya: 'Main criterion — PLAIN, SENSIBLE, EFFICIENT — GLAMOUR A POSITIVE DISADVANTAGE'. It had seemed an intriguing challenge at the time but now it seemed oddly perverse, especially since she'd met

Cade Chamberlayne. Many high powered men, in her experience, flattered their egos by surrounding themselves with beautiful and glamorous women, and there seemed an abundance available through Cosmogems, but evidently Cade Chamberlayne didn't come into the 'most men' category. It was a relief to remember that he'd be away for the first few days in her new job. She loosened her tightly drawn back hair a little.

Lexi reported to Madeleine Honeywell's office well before eight thirty and was surprised to find James Chamberlayne and a handsome, dark-haired woman, already drinking coffee there.

Madeleine was looking worried, but greeted her warmly. 'You're nice and early. Have a coffee, and then we'll go over our general procedures, and I'll show you where everything that you might have to get your hands on actually is when Mr James and Miss Bella have finished their late breakfast,' she added pointedly, clearly disapproving of their laziness.

James, smiling, stood up and shook Lexi's hand. 'Hello again, glad you're joining us. Bella, this is Lexi Brooke, Cade's new PA, Lexi — Bella Weston, my niece, head of Cosmogems editorial department.'

The dark-haired woman remained seated, acknowledging Lexi with the merest nod, and a frigid smile which never reached her blue eyes. She said curtly, 'I hope she fares better than her predecessors,' before turning back to Cade's secretary. 'Look, Madeleine, we need these figures for next months publicity blurb . . . '

'But Cade said he wanted to check them through before general release. He needs to . . . ' She bit her lip.

Bella interjected impatiently. 'He's not here though, is he? He'll be wowing Cosmogems U.S.A. Division at this very moment, so — Cade won't know . . .

This time a deep male voice cut across the argument. 'What exactly won't Cade know, Bella?'

'Cade!' All three gaped in amazement, as he flung open the office door and strode into the room.

'You should be in San Diego,' Bella accused.

'What happened?' Madeleine gasped simultaneously.

Cade's reply was grim. 'I missed my plane on Friday. An accident on the M25 and I was late leaving here.' He threw Lexi an unfriendly look.

She was about to retort that it wasn't her fault, but Madeleine, sensing undercurrents of tension, said quickly, 'Couldn't you have caught another plane?'

He looked at her impatiently. 'I did actually think of that, Maddy. Give me some credit — I spent most of Friday night hanging about Heathrow. There's a trade convention on in San Francisco — not a plane seat to be had at any price. I did try — believe me.'

Lexi could well imagine the uproar Cade could cause when he was bent on getting his own way. His powerful energy was irresistible — in the small office it was almost overwhelming.

'I'd already missed the Friday appointment so, after midnight, I called it a day. I've spent the week-end rearranging the schedule. Fortunately, the actual convention doesn't start until this evening. There's a plane at noon.'

Lexi noted how well the light grey business suit moulded to his broad shoulders and lean hips. Her mouth was dry — she took a sip of coffee, glad he was going away.

The cup clattered back on to its saucer when she heard him say, 'Miss Brooke you've got about two hours to get ready. My chauffeur's outside — he'll take you to your flat to pack, then to the airport. I'll meet you there.'

He turned to James and his niece, frowning. 'What are you two doing here? Monday morning — don't you have departmental meetings to run?'

They both put down their coffee cups and moved swiftly to the door. Bella glowered at Cade and left without a word.

'Just having a chat with Madeleine, checking everything's OK.' James was placatory, even as he sidled out of the office. 'Have a good trip, Cade — sorry about the plane . . . ' He, too, was gone, leaving Cade to stare thoughtfully after his two relatives.

He shrugged and moved across to a computer terminal in the corner of the office and punched the keys. 'Figures for October, Madeleine — I'll take a recent print-out with me.'

'Bella wanted them . . . ' his secretary started to explain, but Cade saw Lexi still sitting there. She'd been fascinated by the interplay of family tensions.

He said, 'Not gone yet? You don't have time to waste — and pack something formal — there's a reception on Wednesday evening. Otherwise . . . ' the shrewd gaze raked over her, 'the sort of thing you're wearing now — plain and sensible.'

Lexi thought there was a hint of irony

in his tone, and her heart sank. Had he seen through her already? But, if so, why carry on with the charade? And how could she refuse to go? 'But . . . I'm not . . . ' she started to protest.

'What now?' Cade didn't look round from his intent study of the V.D.U. screen. 'You're ticket's booked. I presume from previous globe trottings that your passport's in order. What are you waiting for?'

'But — I've been here for less than an hour. I don't know . . . '

'Don't keep butting. It's very irritating. You took the job. You are my personal assistant. A PA on this trip will be very useful so there's no more to be said. Unless you want to quit right now.'

Lexi took a deep breath. He'd flung her a lifeline, though from his expression it would be a red hot one — an uncomfortable few minutes on the receiving end of his blistering tongue, then she'd be off the premises, free to start again — as Lexi Brooke herself, not the prissy caricature she and Anya had wished on her. With a nervous gesture, she resettled her glasses on her nose and opened her mouth to tell him that was fine by her — she'd quit.

Defiantly, she looked at his broad back, muscles loosely bunched under the expensive cloth of his jacket. Then, as though conscious of her stare, he slowly turned round to face her. There was something in his eyes which stopped her speaking. The topaz flecks of liquid amber were prominent in a dark green setting — but it was their mesmerising power which stopped her breath. She felt faint, without the will to speak. It was as though she was totally naked to the soul, without disguise or deception. Cade Chamberlayne was looking into her heart and she felt a powerful squeeze of emotion.

His voice, calm and even, belied the power and perception of his look, but it was still commanding. 'Miss Brooke, I should hate to miss this plane also because of you . . . ' The threat hung heavy in the charged air between them.

Lexi snapped her brain back into action; now it was too late to turn back. 'I'll be there on time.' She stood up and was careful to walk to the door with short precise steps.

Not that Cade Chamberlayne noticed. The spell broken, he was once more absorbed by the graph and bar charts flickering across the green screen. As she closed the door, she heard him say to his secretary, 'I don't like it — there has to be a mistake somewhere. Can you get James back in here, right away.'

* * *

Lexi had never travelled First Class before. It had surprised her that Cade hadn't relegated her to Economy, but the luxury tone had been set as soon as she'd left the office. In Reception, a uniformed chauffeur had stepped forward. 'Lexi Brooke?' It was a confirmation, not a question. 'Don't worry,' he smiled at her surprise, 'Mr

Chamberlayne described you — unmistakeable.'

Lexi hadn't wanted to follow that one up — but would have given a lot to know exactly how she'd been described.

The sleek Mercedes had taken her to the flat. She'd packed a bag, left a note for Anya, and was at Heathrow ten minutes before her boss arrived. He hardly spoke a word as they were processed from check in, through security, and into the first class section of the Boeing 747. Even now, as she began to enjoy the comfort of top exective travel, he was absorbed in a wad of print-out and papers. What he read evidently displeased him. The silence was grim, and his brows furrowed in concentration.

As soon as they were airborne, the cossetting cabin staff offered drinks. Lexi would have loved the champagne, but Cade ordered whisky for himself and orange juice for her. Suitable for Hetty, she thought.

She glanced at the profile beside her; his eyes were cast down on to his papers, and she noticed how long and thick his dark lashes were. His mouth was tightly set and there was a tension in the athletic body which betrayed to her a sense of unease, of something wrong. He read on, swiftly skim reading sheet after sheet. A tiny pulse began to beat at the base of his throat. Lexi imagined touching it; the essence and energy of the whole man would pulsate strongly beneath her fingers. It would be like plugging into an electric socket. Her fingers began to burn — she looked away and picked up a magazine she had bought at the airport.

'I think we can use your time to better purpose than that.' Cade's voice was ominously close to her ear. 'This isn't a holiday trip. You may as well start work straight away.'

'There's nothing I'd like better.' She closed the magazine with a snap. 'But until you give me some guide-lines . . . '

'I've plenty of material here you can

study. And you could try using your initiative.'

Lexi flushed. 'I'll be pleased to use my initiative — when I know more about the job — and what exactly you expect from me.' She tried to keep her voice even, but resentment snagged its edges, remembering how he had put her down when she'd ventured an opinion after the interview. 'What can I do?' she challenged him.

'Plenty.' He stood up, stepping into the aisle, reaching up to the overhead locker. His body blocked her vision, and her eyes were drawn to his slim waist and hard, lean thighs. The expensive material of his clothes enhanced the fluid grace of his muscles so that the simple movement of stretching up and swinging down a leather briefcase, disturbed Lexi as much as his unreasonable demand that she should start work without giving her anything to do! Unease passed through her. Cade Chamberlayne was big — too powerful and dominant for her to cope with as Miss Prim. Her plain, self-effacing librarian victim character would be no match for him. She was afraid her own personality would burst its lid, quite unlike 'plain and sensible' Miss Brooke. Maybe she should begin to assert herself a little, and gradually inject a little steel into her persona.

'Here.' Cade slid back into the seat beside her and tossed the briefcase into her lap. 'This is yours — all the information you'll ever need on Cosmogems, and plenty of background on this trip. I intend to have my pound of flesh — and more. You'll have no time for sight seeing, in fact, you probably won't see anything other than the inside walls of the Arlington Plaza.' The words seemed to give him a lot of satisfaction as he looked down at the top of her mousy brown hair. He added, with relish, 'Don't expect to be part of the glamorous jet set — you'll be on the side lines.'

Lexi decided that now was the time

to add a new dimension to Miss Prim. She picked up the case, noting with surprise, not only its soft expensive leather, but her own initials, L.V.B., engraved in gold letters in the corner! It would make a good souvenir when Cade Chamberlayne sacked her, as he undoubtedly would in the near future. She stiffened her back and looked up at him, tinted spectacles flashing angrily as she spoke, her voice cutting as glass shards.

'Mr Chamberlayne, I told you at the interview that it's not the glamour attached to Cosmogems that attracted me. You don't have a monopoly on that. There are . . . '

He cut in swiftly, his voice taut. 'What was it then?' His green eyes were blazing with anger and suspicion, an over-reaction which shook her. Perhaps he'd seen through her. But did her deception warrant such anger? It wasn't exactly criminal — a mere adjustment of personality. And, if he did suspect her, why bother to bring her on this business trip?

She said, more mildly, hoping to diffuse the rage, 'I was attracted to Cosmogems by its track record. You've hauled it up from a small family business to a formidable company. I . . . I was interested in working for you — to see how you operated — how you ran the company, how . . . ' She tailed off, willing herself to hold Cade's piercing scrutiny, but because she wasn't telling the whole truth, her eyes wavered, and she lowered them to her lap. She did want to work for Cosmogems, but didn't feel it wise to admit that she also wanted to study it as a role model for starting her own business one day!

'You seemed to know rather a lot about Cosmogems before you started.' His voice was still hostile, and his expression was wary, but some of the anger had died, although his eyes were still sightly clouded with suspicion.

Lexi said, rather desperately, 'Surely, if you go for an interview, if you want a job, don't you research the company you want to work for?'

'I wouldn't know. It's a long time since I've worked anywhere but Cosmogems.'

'Well, not you, of course — you're the boss, but . . . ' she hesitated, 'for instance, a vital question would be to know whether a company's healthy — not about to go bankrupt in the near future. There wouldn't be much point in joining a firm on the road to liquidation . . . '

The rest of the sentence was cut off as Cade turned in his seat and took hold of her shoulders, pulling her round to face him. His strong fingers dug into her and she felt a hot tide of feeling. Dark eyes bored into her and she saw, with a jolt of shock, the topaz flecks were huge and hot. Breathing was difficult, but she managed to gasp out, 'Mr Chamberlayne, let me go. What do you think you're doing?'

She tried to shake free, but the vice only tightened, and now the voice was soft with menace. 'And just what have you found out, Miss Brooke, about Cosmogems liquidity?'

'Nothing,' she cried out. 'Nothing. You're a sound, profitable company. I took the job didn't I? And let me go, you're hurting me.'

There was a long pause before he spoke. 'So you did, Miss Brooke, so you did. You took the job — or else you wouldn't be here now — would you?' He was breathing hard but gradually he relaxed his grip, although his hands seemed reluctant to leave her shoulders. The frantic, angry pressure went, the fingers softened, almost stroking the thin material of her suit. He took his hands away, but Lexi felt the heat there for long minutes afterwards.

She released her breath carefully. Not only was Cade Chamberlayne dangerously attractive, he was also volatile, disturbing, and capable of powerfully passionate anger. In the air-conditioned cocoon of first class luxury, thirty thousand feet up, Lexi felt something unusually alien to her — the adrenalin of fear.

He leaned back in his seat, still watching her carefully, although the long lashed brilliant eyes were shuttered. His voice was controlled, but there was a bitter edge of sarcasm when he spoke. 'Well, I'm sure Cosmogems is honoured by your choice — Lexi.' His use of her christian name was not friendly. 'I hope we'll be able to continue to be worthy of that choice. You must tell me if you think we're going wrong in any direction.'

He was so patronisingly snide, so full of mistrust, that Lexi's fear vanished. She didn't have to take this. There were plenty more jobs to be had. She'd occasionally suffered physical insults in her varied careers, but never experienced such mental antagonism; she didn't see why she should put up with it now. So what if her harmless deception had backfired? When she'd made mistakes before, her policy had always been to cut her losses and start again.

She turned to face Cade.

'I can see we are not going to have an ideal working relationship,' she snapped, matching his sarcasm. 'I cannot imagine why you appointed me to be your personal assistant, but to do the job properly, I need your respect, and your trust. You don't seem prepared to give that, so I'm handing in my resignation — as of this moment. We both appear to have made a mistake.' Slapping the case he'd given her back onto his lap, she stood up and glared down at him.

He looked up and his eyes narrowed — she suddenly seemed much taller! A frown started in his eyes, but then, to her amazement, his eyes crinkled and he let out a hoot of amused laughter. 'And where do you imagine you're going to go? A dignified exit from a Boeing 747 in mid-Atlantic is a bit difficult. And you can't even get into the aisle unless I move. I've got you trapped, Lexi!' His mood had changed and he reached for her arm again. 'Sit down, they'll be serving dinner soon.'

'No, thank you.' Lexi's own anger was still boiling. 'Let me pass. I'll find another seat.'

'You'll be lucky. I had a job booking these two. Someone had to be bumped.'

'I'll find a seat in Economy then.'

Cade responded by lifting his hand fractionally. Immediately an attractive hostess appeared. 'Mr Chamberlayne?'

The girl's smile was spaniel-like, Lexi thought in irritation. Still trapped, standing up and unable to move, she remembered to shrink back into her flat 'sensible' shoes.

'Miss Brooke is not happy with her seat on this flight. Can you find her an alternative? Anywhere will do — Economy?'

The pretty face registered shock — horror that anyone should want to forgo the pleasure, not only of first class travel, but of Cade Chamberlayne's company, and she stared disapprovingly at Lexi. 'I'm sorry, Mr Chamberlayne, we'd do anything to help you, you know that, but there isn't a free seat on the plane.' She looked worried. 'Unless she wants to exchange with someone in Economy, that shouldn't be a problem.' She ventured, 'Is there something wrong with the seat itself — perhaps the engineer . . . '

It was impossible for her to accept that someone may hate the company of Cade Chamberlayne fumed Lexi, still awkwardly standing up, furious with Cade, who seemed to be enjoying every moment of this diversion.

'No, Jane, don't worry, I'm sure Miss Brooke will be able to settle down if she puts her mind to it. Perhaps some of your champagne would ease the difficulty.'

'Of course.' The stewardess scuttled off, relieved to have been let off the hook.

Lexi looked enviously at her retreating back.

'Like to change places with Jane?' Cade said lazily, watching her shrewdly.

She sat down abruptly. That's exactly what she had been thinking! 'I remember you had a spell as an air hostess.'

It was infuriating, but there was no choice, Lexi had to stay put and just make the best of it. But the minute the trip was over and they were back in England Cosmogems and Cade Chamberlayne wouldn't see her for dust, however alluring the job. She'd made a fool of herself with her impetuous gesture — a gesture that was pure Lexi Brooke. Now it looked as though she'd have to stay with Hetty Smythe for a while.

Jane returned with a bottle of Dom Perignon and two fluted glasses, leaving it for Cade to pour. Lexi knew she should refuse — it wasn't in Miss Prim's character to drink champagne, but she was sorely tempted, and made only the faintest gesture of demur. 'Thank you, Mr Chamberlayne,' she said, trying to restore her dignity, as he filled her glass.

'Please,' he murmured, turning to

raise his glass to hers, 'call me Cade, if we're to establish the 'ideal working relationship'! I'm sure this will make you forget such nonsense as resigning.'

Lexi sipped as primly as she could, but its sparkling effervescence had a relaxing effect — combined with the fact she'd had nothing to eat but a bowl of Muesli at breakfast, and that already seemed weeks ago! She must keep a tight hold on her brain — Cade Chamberlayne was up to something. The man was exerting all his charm now to beguile her — a swift, inexplicable change of mood!

He settled back with a sigh. 'That's better. Nothing like good champagne to relax the tensions, Lexi.'

'No,' she muttered, uncertain how to respond to this new mood.

'Here.' He returned the briefcase. 'You can study this in your spare time during the next few days, not that there'll be much, but I daresay you can squeeze in a few hours when I don't require your services.'

Lexi thought she imagined a momentary gleam of ambiguity in the green eyes, but his look couldn't have been more innocent, as he spoke rapidly, and objectively — the perfect business briefing, outlining the programme for the next few days. 'It's a two-part trip. First in San Diego, there's a convention of the world's leading cosmetic houses.' His face darkened as he went on. 'Years ago, it was purely scientific, to pool ideas for improved skin care, research into allergies, different forms of laboratory testing. Cosmogems was one of the first companies to drop animal testing . . . '

'Yes, I know,' Lexi interrupted. 'That was one of the reasons for choosing your company. It seemed to have its ethics right.'

He nodded. 'We had to set an example and the convention was a good forum place in those days — all sorts of things were discussed, ideas exchanged — it was held in Chicago then. Unfortunately, the glamour element began to creep in. The science of skin care was overwhelmed by all the glitzy media hype of the cosmetic side of the industry.' He spoke bitterly. 'Now, it's almost worse than a film festival. See and be seen, and the house with the highest profile gets all the media attention — and all the publicity. The art of skin care, and treatment for its deseases, which is what my great aunt Elizabeth believed in, is relegated to a back room. The event's become a circus — even moved its location to San Diego — to give it the glamorous Southern Californian image.' He paused and took a sip of champagne, looking at Lexi sombrely over the rim of his glass. 'I'm going to try and redress the balance this year. That's one of the reasons I want you along. You'll take notes on all the meetings and the seminars. But you'll also be analysing data, looking at the competition, assessing their promotions. You'll have all the equipment you'll need. Here's my schedule.'

He handed her a sheet of paper;

scanning it quickly, she saw he was to be occupied practically every second of every day and every evening. 'There's an awful lot of socialising — parties, receptions, lunches . . . '

'Don't I know it — waste of time, money and effort, but Cosmogems has to complete in the high profile stakes. Usually, James goes to these things, but . . . '

'Yes,' prompted Lexi, as he paused for a long time.

'Well . . . ' Cade seemed reluctant to expand, adding shortly, 'James is excellent at socialising.'

And probably not too hot on skincare or competitor analysis, Lexi decided. The champagne was making her sleepy; she stifled a yawn.

'Hectic week-end?'

The harmless sounding query was swift and Lexi nearly nodded in automatic reflex, then pulled herself up sharply.

'No,' she brushed him off, changing the subject. 'And the second part of the trip?'

His expression changed and a half smile chased away the darkness. 'Ah, that's much more to my taste. We're going to Mexico — but I'll tell you about that later. We can both use some reading time now.'

Obediently, Lexi unzipped the brief-case and pulled out a folder, and they both read in silence as the plane droned on across the land mass of North America. As the cabin lights were dimmed, Cade continued to read, keeping the shaded light away from Lexi, who had finally put away her new briefcase and settled down to sleep. Aware that her identity would be vulnerable to the sharp eyed, wakeful man by her side, she'd swathed herself to the chin in a blanket, put on a sleeping mask, and turned away from him on the reclining seat. It was all well for her peace of mind that she couldn't see the shrewdly speculative looks Cade Chamberlayne gave her from time to time throughout the night.

3

The first class V.I.P. treatment continued. A chauffeur driven limousine whisked them from the airport to the luxurious Arlington Plaza Hotel in San Diego City. Cosmogems was host to the convention and Cade had ordered the top floor penthouse to be set up as headquarters.

'That's fine.' He nodded approval as he prowled around the large rooms.

The hotel manager relaxed and prepared to leave. 'Enjoy your visit, Mr Chamberlayne. Perhaps you'll see something of the city?'

'It's doubtful,' Cade frowned, 'this is a working trip.' He was already switching on computers, banked in a corner of the extensive living area.

'Your room's through there.' He indicated to Lexi a door on the right. 'Unpack, freshen up, and let's start.'

She went without a word. Since her moments of rebellion on the plane she'd assumed the role of obedient employee — she could think of no other way to survive the next few days, and there were compensations, she realised as she examined her huge room, with its king size bed and palatial bathroom, complete with Jacuzzi. The four walls of the Arlington plaza would do her very well!

'I said freshen up, not a remodelling job,' Cade called impatiently.

Very appropriate, Lexi mused, pulling a wry face at her reflection in the mirror tiled bathroom.

'Just one moment,' she replied sweetly. Jet lag was foreign to her, and the adrenaline of challenge was racing through her veins. She felt keyed up, anxious to throw herself into work, to deflect Cade's personal scrutiny. The first problem was clothes — she hadn't thought past the interview and the first few days at Cosmogems. Plain and sensible wasn't the keynote of her stylish and colourful wardrobe! She quickly changed her travelling suit for a simple, black skirt and the plainest shirt she'd been able to find. But the 'plain shirt' was a striking jade green, the folds of which clung to her figure. The mirror told her it wouldn't do — it was just the opposite of plain and sensible! There was an impatient knock on the door and she desperately pulled on a roomy, coverall, black sweater — just in time!

Cade stood in the doorway, frowning. 'What on earth are you doing. We've just an hour to set up for the reception and first session. I hope you usually work faster than this.'

'Yes, I do. I'm ready.' She looked at him, defiance hidden behind large spectacles.

The look he returned was appraising, lingering on the black sweater, and Lexi had the feeling that she was being subjected to an X-ray examination. She stilled her breath as his eyes narrowed, but the moment passed.

'Come on — Cosmogems U.S.A.

representatives will be here soon. It's time you met some collagues.'

* * *

The next three days were among the most stimulating of Lexi's life. In seventy-two hours of close working proximity with Cade and his American staff she learned more about business than on her entire college course.

Cade was a fascinating operator to watch. All things to all occasions, he was a charismatic host and a witty and charming speaker, giving Cosmogems a high, glamorous profile amongst some of the glitziest companies in the world. He was at every presentation, every working lunch and dinner, driving Lexi at a relentless pace, expecting her to accompany him and present a detailed analytical report of the proceedings afterwards. They worked into the early hours, no hint of antagonism between them, her quick mind racing along with his, as she prepared endless data and notes for speeches.

The convention highlight was Cade's address on skin care. His style and dedication took Lexi's breath away. She'd had no idea of the depth of his commitment to the problems of skin allergies, disfigurements and diseases. Sweeping his audience along with him, he made a passionate plea for time and money to be spent on research, rather than poured into more and more advertising and the duplication of cosmetic products. It was a dangerous concept to put forward to such a highly profit conscious gathering, but Cade held his initially sceptical audience, and Lexi found herself on her feet, applauding with the rest of them at the end.

'Congratulations — that was a wonderful speech,' she told him as they finally returned to the living-room of the penthouse.

Cade shrugged off his jacket, loosened his tie, and opened the well-stocked mini-bar. 'Thanks — drink?' he offered.

'Yes — oh, no, thank you.' Lexi remembered in time, though with the euphoric high of the speech still with her, a glass of wine would have been perfect.

'You don't mind if I do?'

'You're the boss.' Lexi was surprised he considered it necessary to ask her permission. Perched on the edge of an armchair, she waited for Cade to dictate his thoughts on the days's meetings. It had become a regular feature of her job, and she looked forward to the stimulation of his analysis. More secure in her disguise, she was beginning to relax. It was becoming second nature to be up at dawn, checking make-up and hair, and she was beginning to dismiss her fears that he suspected she had a persona other than that of Hetty Smythe!

The next day would be the last day of the convention, and they they were moving on to Mexico. Cade, relaxed after his success, poured a small whisky into an ice filled tumbler, and wandered over to the ceiling-to-floor glass window overlooking the city. He had his back to Lexi, one hand thrust deep into his pocket. She waited, eyes drawn to the powerful grace of his body silhouetted against the black window.

'Come here, Lexi,' he said softly.

Her breath caught in her throat. The room was very quiet, suspended high above the town. 'What for?'

He didn't turn. 'Just come over here. Please.'

She went to stand near him.

He laughed. 'What's the matter? Why are you scared? I only want to show you the view.'

'I'm not scared.' But she hated the squeaky pitch of her voice.

'Well then . . . ' He placed a casual arm on her shoulders to move her closer as he pointed to the skyline. 'Look — diamonds in the sky — the lights of the Coronado Bridge. And the aeroplanes — busy little shining glow worms.'

'Glow worms!' Lexi, very much aware of the light pressure of his hand on her shoulder, was astonished. 'Glow worms' in this context didn't accord with the hard headed business man performance she'd witnessed during the past few days.

'I'd give those jewels for a set of beads,' he quoted. 'The city lights, cars, streetlamps — they're pretty, sparkling falsehoods, outshining the natural beauty of the stars. In Mexico, I'll show you the real gems of the desert in the night sky. They're true, authentic. I hate sham — deception of any kind. Those lights down there confuse the truth.' He turned his head to look directly at her, the strong face relaxed, younger looking, the topaz flecks more pronounced. His lips parted in a half smile and Lexi shivered.

'What's wrong?' he asked quietly.

'Nothing — I didn't realise you were . . . ' Her voice tailing off in confusion, she made a small sideways movement to escape, but his fingers tightened their grip.

'You didn't realise I was what?' Cade

was menacingly innocent as he held her gaze. 'Things aren't always what they seem — don't you find that? Those car headlights down there look like jewels from up here. You and I know they're not.'

Lexi was uncomfortable. What was he driving at?

'They're pretty enough — but I'd like to get on with your work, if we're to finish this tonight.'

'Of course.' He smiled again, and Lexi's heart raced. He was in the strangest of moods. The green and topaz eyes were superficially friendly, but there was something unnerving in their depths. She looked away, her shoulders and neck were tense and aching, her fingers stiff from the keyboard. Moving away from him, she sat down at her desk, flexing her forearms, rubbing her neck.

Cade looked up from his notes. 'A problem?'

'No,' she answered shortly. 'Stiff, that's all.'

To her surprise, he dropped the papers on the sofa and ran a hand though his thick hair. She noticed that the curls, ruffled to an attractive disorder, lent a vulnerability to his strong face.

'I'm a brute. I've worked you too hard. Mexico will be easier.' His smile was friendly. 'You've done well — I couldn't have managed without you.'

Stop it — Lexi screamed inside, totally confused by his behaviour. The caring, vulnerable, poetic role was uncharacteristic. Why was he playing it? She had an urgent desire to escape, and half rose, but Cade was swifter. Behind her chair, he placed his hands on her shoulders. The fine hairs on the nape of her neck prickled as he started to massage her back.

'No.' She tensed, tried to move away.

He laughed. 'Relax — don't make things difficult. This will help — my speciality. Lean back, stop fighting. You've worked hard — you deserve a reward.'

The effect of the strong hands was

immediate, ironing out the knotted muscle and clenched ligaments. His thumbs rotated and probed round tension spots she didn't know she had. Instinctively, she began to relax, feeling softer and heavier under the calming expert hands. If felt so good, she leaned back, her head falling against Cade's broad chest, as the measured movements halted fractionally before they continued down her back, separating and kneading each vertebrae, moving up to the base of the skull.

'You've done this before,' she breathed, recognising an expert.

'Frequently.' His slow voice was lazy, keeping time with the rhythmic motions.

The tension had gone, but Lexi couldn't move. She wanted the hands to go on — and on — forever — soothing, stroking . . . Cade's hands slowed as she relaxed against him. Warm langour turned her bones and limbs to jelly. She was no longer Lexi Brooke or Hetty Smythe — merely clay to be moulded by Cade's dominant hands. He held her face, tracing the contours of her neck and jaw. Looking up, she saw Cade's face above hers, and his look of intensity burned into her brain and body. Her own hands lifted towards him. Then she heard his voice — so low, she had to strain to hear what he said.

'I say again, Miss Brooke, appearances can be deceptive.' She imagined that his lips brushed her ear, but his next words were loud and clear. As he took away his hands, he said, briskly, 'That should do the trick. Now, if you'd like to knock my notes into a report, we'll check it through in the morning. Good-night, Miss Brooke.' With one enigmatic glance, he picked up his whisky glass and went into his bedroom.

★ ★ ★

The bubbling Jacuzzi jets pummelled Lexi's body but did nothing to quieten her jumping nerves. 'Hetty Smythe, what have you done?' she groaned, sinking lower into the foaming water, trying to drown the memory of those last few minutes with Cade Chamberlayne, when she'd allowed herself to be so spineless under his hands, allowing him to take her off guard. He must have been aware of the effect he was having on her, and she would have to see that knowledge in his eyes every time she looked at him.

But what was his purpose? A perverse satisfaction in teasing old-maidish Hetty? A boost to the male ego? It didn't seem at all likely that a man like Cade would have to stoop to such lengths to get his kicks. 'Power crazed,' Lexi snorted, full of anger at him and herself. She'd make sure she wouldn't be caught out again!

It was nearly dawn before she fell into a restless doze, broken by dreams that she was Hetty Smythe, the librarian, pursued by all the demons of hell, intent on her murder!

Washed out and weary, she dreaded meeting Cade next morning but, to her perverse irritation, he barely glanced at her as she joined him for orange juice and coffee.

'Reports finished?' he asked, off-handedly, immersed in the financial papers.

'Of course,' she answered tartly, but her heart gave a painful leap as she looked at his tall figure, lounging in the chair she'd sat in the evening before, feeling his fingers on her spine . . .

He looked full of crackling, dynamic energy, as he picked up the day's schedule. 'Not much left for today — plenary session, fashion show.' He pulled a face. 'Final reception this evening. Should be time for a look round Old Town, San Diego. I'll take you there this afternoon. We can get out of the fashion show.'

'No thanks,' Lexi snapped, 'I'd like to go to the fashion show, and I've some shopping to do.' You don't catch me again, she thought, looking at him coldly. You're too dangerous, Cade Chamberlayne, so keep your distance.

He shrugged. 'Please yourself — your loss,' he said smugly.

Lexi bit her lip — she hated the way her heart was beating out an uncertain wayward rhythm. 'What do we do in Mexico?' she asked, desperate to change the subject.

'Mexico will be different . . . ' The phone interrupted him and he gestured to Lexi to take it.

'It's for you. James Chamberlayne. He says it's urgent.' She carried the phone over to Cade, checking her watch. Eight o'clock — midnight in England. She wondered what was so urgent. There had been an odd note in James' voice — panic? — fear?

From Cade's expression, it could only be bad news. A thunderous expression darkened his face, and his knuckles whitened as he gripped the handset. Listening grimly, he interrupted James occasionally with a sharp question. Finally he said, 'I'll be back tomorrow. Don't do anything until I get back. No!' The exclamation was whip-lash. 'I said don't do anything. I'll handle it. You appear to have done enough damage. Lexi will fax our flight time. Be sure you meet that plane. I want all the details. Just be there!' He slammed down the phone, black anger in his eyes.

'What is it?' Lexi asked nervously, feeling the force of his rage still vibrating round the room.

'That cousin of mine! Why can't he do anything properly? I have to take charge of every last detail — he just can't seem to . . . ' He broke off, shaking his head. 'Sorry, forget I said that. It's nothing to do with you. It's a family matter.'

'But it is to do with me, if I'm your personal assistant.' She burst out hotly, 'How can I do my job unless I know what goes on?'

'Maybe you're right,' he conceded, to her surprise, 'but just look after things here today. Don't miss a thing, especially at the reception. I'll go to Mexico now, if I can rearrange the appointments — again!' He started stuffing files and papers in his brief case. 'Cancel Friday's flight and book the first one tomorrow, fax James . . . '

'Yes, I heard. Cosmogems?' She faced him. 'Am I allowed to know what's happened there — or is that a family secret, too?' she added acidly.

'You'll know soon enough when we get back, but I may as well tell you now.' He rubbed his hand across his forehead and, for a second, the thrusting, energetic entrepreneur disappeared, and Lexi glimpsed a man worried by a heavy burden he was carrying alone. 'Would you pour me some coffee please — black. I'm going to need it today. Cosmogems?' He shrugged bitterly. 'James was in charge of launching an important new range of skin care products next week — with all the usual razmattaz — advertising campaign, top TV star endorsement etc. It was top secret — tightest security we've ever had. Last night Lennox launched exactly the same range — and at a cheaper price. Effectively killed months, no — years of work. How could it have happened?'

'I'm sorry.' Lexi's anger had cooled.

'So am I! We'll have to go back tomorrow. See what I can pull out of the wreck — maybe revamp the campaign . . .

'Can I help . . . ?'

'Of course. What do you think I'm paying you for. It'll be damned hard work, but I'll think of something.' He gulped down his coffee and slung his jacket over his shoulder. At the door he paused. 'What a pity I won't be able to show you those night gems of the desert.' His voice was soft, his eyes enticing.

Lexi frowned — it was an act. She recognised a good, little cameo part when she saw one. Cat and mouse game — trying to provoke a response in her. Frigidly, she doused the expression on his face. 'I don't think that would be at all appropriate — Sir.' It was her best Hetty Smythe voice.

She heard him laugh as he left the room and glared after him, furious that the image of a starry desert night with Cade had started her nerve ends tingling. At the same time as she hated him for that, she couldn't help inhaling the male scent of soap and tangy aftershave as he left the room. Even when he wasn't there, his presence filled the empty space. For several minutes she sat quite still, pushing away the disturbing evidence of her senses, telling herself that what was happening to her was just not possible.

4

Those were the last quiet moments of the day and Lexi had little time to agonise over her feelings for Cade. She was far too busy covering the day's meetings, compiling a report on the entire convention and analysing the fashion show from the cosmetic and jewellery angle. It was nearly eight o'clock before she looked up from her desk. The reception! Cade wasn't back. She had to go — it was a valuable time for picking up scraps of information, making contacts — the final hour when inhibitions and tongues would be loosened.

She showered and changed at top speed. This was the formal occasion Cade had mentioned. She'd planned to wear a dark skirt and severe high-necked shirt — a plain enough combination but, to her exasperation, she found in her hasty packing she'd picked up the wrong shirt — a creamy silk with a deeply plunging neckline. She prayed Cade wouldn't be back — the reception was for cocktails only and shouldn't last longer than an hour. Mexico was only twenty miles or so across the border, but he hadn't told her exactly where he was going.

A quick check in the mirror, and Lexi added a gold pendant with a pearl drop — to detract from her revealing neckline, but in fact, the effect of the softly lustrous jewel nestling in the hollow of her throat was more startlingly attractive than she realised, and in spite of the muted make-up and severe hair style, the girl who entered the Arlington Plaza Ballroom was more Lexi Brooke than Hetty Smythe!

There was a frisson of interest as she circulated amongst the glitzy assembly, but she refused all attempts to press alcohol on her. She needed a clear head and her brain registered all the information useful to Cosmogems, and the many complimentary comments on Cade's speech.

In five minutes she reckoned she could return to the safe anonymity of her room to finish her reports. The crowd had thinned, but as she turned to go, Cade came in with a group of people. He was in evening dress and looked overpoweringly handsome as he smiled down at the well groomed and bejewelled woman who was holding his arm. Lifting his head, he scanned the room, eyes narrowing when he saw Lexi, who remembered, just in time, to sink down into her flatish shoes.

Disengaging his arm, Cade walked across, eyes taking her in from head to foot, finally focussing on the pearl at her throat. Lexi rounded her shoulders and put up her hand to cover her chest. His lip curved, but the smile never reached his eyes. 'Still working?' The question was innocent, the emphasis on 'working', threatening. She was startled by the outright hostility in the glittering eyes, a dangerous spring of coiled tension in the set of his broad shoulders. He reached out and picked up the pearl, his fingers scorching her skin.

'Don't,' she snapped.

'Why not?' he shot back, holding on to the gold chain. 'Are you frightened I'll find out it's false? Pearls can be very deceptive, as I'm sure you know.' He had drawn her so close that their faces almost touched. Lexi saw white teeth behind the parted lips, noticed the fine silver wires in his black hair, the golden flecks in his eyes amber dark.

She ran her tongue over her lips and Cade's hold tightened, the chain cutting into the back of her neck. The tension between them crackled like static, until a brittle voice cut the wires. 'Cade, darling, come on, we'll be late.' The dark haired woman plucked at his arm, her gold bracelets jangling heavily. Red lips pouted in make-up which was a flawless mask of understated expertise. She barely glanced at Lexi, who was intensely conscious of her own drab make-up and hairstyle.

Cade released his hold and stepped back, but his eyes never left Lexi's face. 'I'm going out to dinner,' he grated. 'I'll expect to see all the paperwork completed when I get back. I'll see you in the morning — Miss Brooke.' The name was flung at Lexi like an accusation, as he took the dark haired woman by the elbow and walked away.

Lexi was stunned by the hurricane force of his anger, and she was at the storm centre. What had happened since the phone call from James to make him so hostile towards her? Suddenly, desperately, she wanted her own identity back — to be able to confront Cade Chamberlayne on her own terms — as his personal assistant, but also as herself, Lexi Brooke — if he didn't like it, he could get rid of her. Ever honest, she admitted his strong attraction — more than for any man she'd met before. Her disguise had trapped her and it was a hindrance she'd no idea how to get rid of. It was impossible to confront Cade in his present angry mood. That would have to wait until they were back in London. If she admitted her deception now, she wouldn't put it past him to fire her on the spot and leave her stranded in San Diego. Well, that wasn't too disastrous a thought — she'd been in far worse spots in her life, though she wouldn't be able to afford the Arlington Plaza!

With a fatalistic sense of what would be, would be, Lexi went towards the lifts. A voice made her turn back.

'Lexi Brooke?' It was tentative and uncertain.

'Peter!' She smiled in pleasure at the shortish, balding man who stepped towards her, cameras festooning his body. 'Where've you come from? I didn't notice you before.'

'Stand in for the last day. Martin had to fly back home — wife's had a baby, premature. I was in Los Angeles, so . . . '

Lexi took his arm, delighted to see an old photographer friend from her brief modelling days. Peter Stephens had always encouraged her, and she'd always trusted him. He had been disappointed when she hadn't pursued a fashion career. The incredulity on his face made her laugh. 'Do I look so bad?'

'No — but there's something odd. I hardly recognise you.'

'Good.'

'Why, Lexi? You've deliberately put out the light. You used to sparkle, set the place on fire.'

She couldn't help giggling. 'You make me sound like an arsonist. This is only temporary. And I'm beginning to regret it.' To his puzzled look, she added, 'I'm acting — the plain and sensible PA without glamour. I toned myself down, got the job, and here I am. As simple as that.' If only that were true, Lex thought ruefully.

Peter gave a low whistle. 'Cade Chamberlayne! You picked a handful there — and Cosmogems!' There was a worried note of doubt in his voice, which Lexi was swift to pick up. She looked enquiringly at him. He hesitated. 'Perhaps I shouldn't say anything . . . I hate rumours . . . but . . .'

'But?' she prompted.

'There's been a whisper that Cosmogems is in trouble. They lost a big jewellery contract, and there seems to be other problems.'

'I've not heard anything.' Lexi cut in sharply.

'How long have you been working for them?'

'Four days,' she admitted reluctantly, 'but I researched them thoroughly. Cade's taken the company to the top of the league.'

'He's certainly done that,' Peter admitted. 'It's just that lately . . . look, I really don't know anything definite. I've got to fly now, literally. Let's meet in London next week. I'll keep my ear to the ground. We'll talk again. Meanwhile, have fun, and bring the old Lexi back next week.' He leaned forward to kiss her cheek. 'On second thoughts, she's still there, of course.'

Lexi waved him off affectionately, and went up to her room. Cosmogems in trouble! Hard to believe, yet Cade did seem strained, acting as though he carried a burden he wasn't able to share. And what was it that Madelaine had been going to say just after her interview? James' phone call — Cade's excessive anger — there were certainly some puzzling factors. She sighed. Just as well, given her unsettling feelings about Cade, that she'd decided to get out of what was proving to have been a disastrous error of judgement on her part.

At least she'd make the most of her last night of luxury at the Arlington Plaza! She took a long Jacuzzi, undid her heavy plait, brushed out her hair, slipped into the short towelling robe provided by the hotel and spread both herself and papers out on the big double bed. Cade wouldn't be back until late, but she didn't want to meet him in the sitting room. Turning on some music, she settled down to work and was soon absorbed in sorting out the mass of material from the convention into a logical and succinct analysis.

Even though she'd only been working for Cosmogems for such a short time, she was convinced it would have led her into the right career move had she been able to stay a while. Her tentative ideas of running her own business had crystalised into a clear cut ambition. It was what she wanted to do, and Cade Chamberlayne was the perfect role model — would have been, she thought sadly, but for that silly advert which had led her into such a predicament.

To finish her work she needed some information from Cade's briefcase which he'd left in the sitting room. She brought it into her room and found the folder she needed. A disc marked 'Confidential' caught her eye. Cade hadn't told her she had free information access on Cosmogems, but he hadn't placed any restrictions either. She hadn't noticed this particular piece of software before, and curiosity made her run it through the computer. As the printer clattered out its facts and figures, Lexi's casual observation sharpened. There was a pattern emerging which didn't make sense.

The information on the disc didn't correlate with information she already had on file. Comprehensive costings between competitors' and Cosmogems' products didn't tally. Puzzled, she took the print-out back to her room to compare with the costings Cade had given her. Totally absorbed, her 'come in' was an automatic response to the knock on the door, but the angry, 'Have you got my briefcase in there?' tested her reflexes as never before. Cade must have come in without her hearing him.

'Yes — wait — don't come in, I'm in the shower,' was a panic stricken improvisation, born out of guilt. Her reflexes didn't let her down. As the door opened, she grabbed a towel and wrapped it round her head. She leapt for the door, briefcase in hand. 'Here.

Sorry, I wanted some papers. I was just going to put it back.' She thrust the case at Cade as he stood in the doorway and tried to slam the door shut, but his reflexes were faster. One foot stopped the door, a powerful shoulder pushing easily against her strength to crash it open. She was flung back against the wall still clutching the case, the towel and robe dropping to the floor unheeded.

Cade took in the disordered bed, the files and papers, and the tall girl with thick tumbled hair against the wall, her wide grey-green eyes fearful, but defiant. The straight, blue nightshirt revealed a figure of breathtaking shapeliness. He took a step towards her, his eyes brilliant with a triumphant excitement. 'What's this?' his voice rasped harshly, 'a private audit of Cosmogems? While the cat's away . . . but you're no mouse. That prim little exterior's just a sham. You're a cat — and a pretty wild cat, I imagine.'

Lexi pressed back against the wall as

97

he moved nearer, his eyes fixed on hers.

'Now you don't have your glasses, your plain shapeless suits, and your flat heels to hide behind, I can see what you're really like.'

'Get out of my room,' Lexi lashed out.

'I've no intention of going — yet. By deception you've forfeited your rights. I want to find out what sort of woman you really are. There's one way I can find out and we both know what it is.' His voice was soft with menace, and Lexi felt a thrill of misgiving.

'Cade . . . ' she began, 'I can explain . . . '

'It's too late.' He put his hands on the wall, pinning her like an impaled butterfly. 'Playing with fire can be dangerous . . . ' He bent his head and took her mouth with confident authority.

Lexi knew what she should do. A basic self-defence move could easily break his hold, but she sensed he would always be one move ahead of her. His hands had already moved down to her waist, imprisoning her even more firmly. The kiss deepened, and a wild burst of sensation set her body on fire — a force she'd never experienced before in her life made her respond, and return his kiss.

He kissed her again. She moaned as his mouth descended on hers; it was a kiss of such shattering intensity and sweet sensation that it must go on for ever. Fighting desperately for control, Lexi brought her hands to his shoulders and pushed, but before she could gasp out 'No', he had moved away from her and stood looking down at her, breathing hard.

'So, that's the kind of woman you are, Lexi Brooke. How far would you go to get me to forget the truth? I expect you've acted this role lots of times! This time it was to be Miss Plain and Sensible, but you couldn't keep it up. The truth came out — eventually. I suspected you were no Miss Prim at the interview.'

Fury, guilt, and a sense of injustice filled Lexi's brain. 'Now you know — just get out. Leave me alone. I never want to see you again.'

Cade folded his arms and leaned against the door frame. 'And if I don't?' he frowned.

'I'll have you thrown out.'

'I'd like to see you try. I distinctly heard you say 'come in', and your night shirt is extremely provoctive.' His eyes looked her over with slow deliberation. 'You're in my employment. Don't forget. You'll do as you're told.'

'Oh, no I won't,' Lexi seethed. 'I don't have to work for you — as soon as I get back to England . . . '

'Not that again, it's boring. To quit a job twice in four days is something of a record, but I always put you down as uncommitted.'

'Why employ me then?'

'Several reasons — I want to know what you're up to, that'll do for the present.'

'I'm not up to anything.' Lexi cried angrily.

'Don't make things worse by lying. No-one goes to the lengths you've gone to, to infiltrate Cosmogems, without there being some very good reasons.'

'You can't make me work for you. I don't have to see you again after tomorrow. You can't keep me working for you.'

'Can't I?' His interjection was clipped. 'I think you'll find that I can.'

'How? We don't live in the slave era. I'm free to go as I please.'

'You obviously belong to the careless breed who don't read the small print of a contract before signing, and then complain when they find themselves trapped. You can't leave Cosmogems for six months. I always put that in contracts for senior staff — as a safeguard. I can get rid of you — any time. But you can't get rid of me. If you try to leave before six months is up, you'll find yourself with a hefty breach of contract suit on your hands. And don't think I wouldn't sue you — it'd be a pleasure. You can only leave when, and if, I choose to release you. Six months should be enough. After that — you can go to the devil.' He glared at her, a look so full of suspicious dislike that Lexi's spirits quailed.

She opened her mouth to protest, but Cade forestalled her. 'Until this morning — and make sure all the work is finished,' he flung at her as he went out, slamming the door behind him.

5

Hetty Smythe was dead and buried, and not a moment too soon, Lexi thought, as she joined a darkly brooding Cade for an early breakfast the following morning. At least now she could be her own straightforward self. Her anger towards Cade had cooled. Objectively, she couldn't blame him for thinking she was up to something — but what possible harm could she do to Cosmogems? She was puzzled and intrigued. If Cade forced her to stay with the firm, she would try to find out what was going on, if only to clear her own reputation.

She refused to recognise the fluttering of her senses as Cade scowled at her across the table. His offer of coffee was more a contemptuous bark than a pleasant early morning invitation.

'Please.' With loosened hair, and freed from the 'Hetty' make-up she looked attractive and vital. Deciding she may as well be hung for the proverbial sheep, she took a deep breath.

'Cade, I want to apologise. I know it must look bad.'

'Damn right,' he interupted grimly, 'it's as bad as possible — for you. It's easier for me now I know what you are, and can put a stop to the game you're playing. What I need to know, is who's behind you?'

'I don't have a game, and no-one's behind me.' Lexi gulped down black coffee. She needed it strong. 'You're totally wrong, the only thing I did was to — er — mislead you a little.'

'A little!' Cade stood up and banged his first on the table, rattling his cup and saucer. 'A little! You walk into my office, purporting to be a prim, colourless . . . '

Lexi stood up to face him, wide grey eyes, without the spectacles, expressive but angry. The coffee had given her courage. 'No. Cade — Mr Chamber-layne — just listen. At least give me a chance to explain. Even a criminal's allowed to muster a defence, and I'm not criminal. Just,' she hesitated, choosing her words carefully, 'perhaps misguided. Please, what can you lose?'

Cade stared at her sombrely, his brow still knitted in a scowl, but he slowly sat down. 'You've got about five minutes before the car arrives. And, I might add, I'm prepared to disbelieve anything you say.'

Lexi shrugged. 'That's your right as prosecutor.' She looked at her watch. 'I don't need five minutes. This is the truth. Last night I wasn't 'spying', 'prying', or whatever. I ran the tape because I was unsure of some figures. I'm sorry if it was confidential.' She hurried on, not wanting to dwell on that. Before she could say anything she needed a clearer picture, and she had to regain Cade's trust. 'The 'Miss Prim' routine, I grant you, was a deception. No,' she put up her hand as Cade looked set to interrupt again. 'My defence is that you deliberately provoked that with your,' she was about to say 'stupid advert', but thought better of it — he was still her boss! 'own misleading advert. It caught my attention, and I was intrigued. After I'd researched Cosmogems, I wanted the job. I wanted to work for you, and figured that a small deception wouldn't do any harm. I was wrong. It was foolish, and I'm sorry. But that's my own fault. You must believe me.' She faced him openly painfully aware how important it was that he believed her.

His eyes were expressionless, his face shuttered. 'You're an excellent actress.' He spoke coldly. 'At first, you had me fooled. I told you at the interview that I wanted an efficient personal assistant, not someone who's trying to gain a way into modelling, via Cosmogems. It's happened too often. That's why the advert was worded like that.'

'I *don't* want to be a model!' Lexi's voice rose in exasperation. 'Look, I didn't put it in my c.v. for obvious reasons, but I've done modelling. I hated it! It's not what I want to do.'

'False representation now! Your c.v. was inaccurate then,' Cade pounded.

But Lexi wasn't giving up — she still had a minute. 'Not inaccurate, just some omissions and, you should know by now, I'm good at the job.' She held his eyes steadily for several seconds.

He returned her look, then glanced down at his watch. 'Your time is up, Miss Brooke. We can't afford to miss the plane. I hope your 'sensible' clothing is packed. You can leave your stage make up in the waste-bin.'

'But you do believe me?'

Cade moved away from the table and went towards his room, his tall figure immaculate in a light grey suit. At his door, he turned. 'There's nothing in my rules to say I have to give you a verdict this morning. You've still got six months hard labour to do. Your hand luggage will be your briefcase. I want all your paperwork on board with you. There'll be no light reading on this trip. I'll meet you in the lobby downstairs in two minutes.'

Lexi poured herself a cup more of the strong coffee, annoyed to find her hands shaking. Damn the man — did he have to look so attractive?

* * *

Cade was as good as his word. Throughout the long plane journey, he worked Lexi relentlessly, going through her reports on the Convention, questioning and assessing. He produced a lap top computer, and gave her a mass of data to analyse and edit. He allowed the briefest of meal breaks, but no sleep. She didn't mind. While they worked together they had a rapport, which was far preferable to Cade's suspicious anger. She enjoyed the work. It was the quickest flight she'd ever experienced.

When the pilot announced the plane was over the United Kingdom land mass, Cade finally relaxed. He took the computer from her. 'That's enough. We'll be at Heathrow soon — take a break.'

'Thanks.' She tried to keep the irony out of her voice.

Cade threw her a keen look. 'I'll give you this — you work hard.' He sounded grudging. 'Tired?'

'No. I like the work — it's what I want to do.' She tidied up papers and print-outs into her briefcase. 'I think Cosmogems is a fascinating company.'

Cade's grunt was ambiguous, but his mouth was relaxed, his eyes marginally less hostile. 'Let's forget Cosmogems for a moment. I need to know about you — personally.'

'It's all in my file in Madeleine Honeywell's office. I'm sure you did your homework before you shortlisted me.' Lexi was defensive. As long as they stuck to work she felt safe. Under the personal spotlight of his scrutiny, she felt a treacherous flutter of her senses. She glanced at him, and wished she hadn't! Leaning back in his seat, a half smile on his face, dark hair only slightly ruffled, he looked as attractive and dynamic as ever. He showed no sign of fatigue, despite the punishing schedule of the past few days. She clenched her muscles — she could tell he was about to slip into his 'charm' mode. She avoided his eye, busied herself with her briefcase, taking out the papers she'd just put away. She jumped as he put his hand on hers.

'What's the problem, Lexi? I said that's enough. You can get back to Cosmogems in the morning.' He put her briefcase on the floor, and continued his assessing scrutiny. 'I need to place you in a context — a personal one.'

'Why? What's my personal life got to do with you?'

'Quite a lot — if whoever, or whatever, you are, is affecting Cosmogems.'

'How could I possibly affect a company such as Cosmogems?' Lexi spoke wearily — he obviously still believed there was a more sinister motive for her deception. 'If you'd tell me what I'm supposed to be up to.'

Cade seemed to come to a decision. He cut in swiftly. 'You'll have to know sometime, although you're probably well aware of the facts already if you are up to something. Cosmogems has suddenly started to go through a bad patch — for no apparent reason. Sales have slipped in the cosmetic and skin care division — our financial bread and butter. Our competitors always seem to be one step ahead, whatever we do. That's why I was persuaded, against my better judgement, to hire you. James is Sales Director, and Mike Simmonds is a first class Financial Director. I usually leave them strictly alone to get on with their jobs. Now I need to scrutinise every department and function of the firm, and I need time for that. You were to provide me with that time — to root out whatever viper or gremlin has got into the system.' The scowl momentarily returned. 'Now it seems there's a distinct possibility that I've hired myself one of the very vipers I'm trying to find. But, I intend to follow the trail.'

Lexi's heart sank, but she spoke firmly. 'You are absolutely one hundred per cent wrong about my involvement with anything or anyone who may be trying to harm your company. If I can't say anything more to convince you, you'll have to take my word for it. I didn't even know Cosmogems was in any trouble until James rang. You appeared to be thriving and prosperous.' She remembered Peter Stephen's words — 'a lost contract, other problems', and vowing to keep silent about what she knew, bit her lip.

Cade looked at her sceptically, but merely lifted his eyebrows. 'You're Miss Brooke on paper. Are you married?'

'No.'

'Have you ever been married?'

'No.'

'Not even nearly?'

'No.'

'Boyfriends?'

'Of course. I am twenty-seven.'

'And very attractive,' Cade commented drily. 'Even Miss Prim couldn't conceal that.'

'Thank you.' Lexi took a breath. 'Are you married?' She was pleased to see he looked started.

'No.' His reply was curt.

'Girlfriends?' Her eyes were wickedly innocent, but she wondered if she'd gone too far when Cade's green eyes hardened, and the topaz flecks began to flame. 'I'm sorry,' she said hastily, 'it's none of my business.'

'No. it isn't. Don't forget I employ you — not the other way round.' Then he startled her even further. A boyish smile replaced the authoritarian put-down look. 'And I'm thirty-six. Draw your own conclusions, Miss Brooke.'

Touché, Lexi thought, a sudden stab of jealousy catching her below the ribs.

London, in a greyish dawn light, looked drab after the glitzy San Diego scene. Lexi adjusted her watch before she stepped out of the plane. It was five o'clock British time and Lexi knew it would take her a short time to adjust.

Cade still radiated a dynamic energy, and looked far fresher than James, who met them at Heathrow with a subdued greeting. After an incredulous look at Lexi's changed appearance, he cast apprehensive glances at his cousin as they walked towards the chauffeur driven limousine which materialised magically outside the airport.

'No hitches there. Well done, James.' Cade was grimly sarcastic. 'How'd you manage it?'

'Don't be like that, Cade. It wasn't my fault — Lennox's . . . '

'Brief me in the car,' Cade snapped, turning to Lexi. 'James and I are going straight to Cosmogems. You take a taxi. Go home, sort yourself out and be at the office as soon as possible.'

Lexi's jaw dropped. Not even a day, or a morning's respite!

He knew exactly what she was thinking. With an exaggerated gesture, he looked at his watch. 'It's Friday — a working day, Lexi — had you forgotten? And don't make any plans for the week-end. Cancel any you've made, in fact.'

'But . . . '

He stopped closer to her, his eyes flashing dangerously. 'No 'buts' — six months hard, don't forget. It started on the plane — it carries on. And,' his full lip curled upwards in a fleeting smile, 'if you recall, we do have an emergency on our hands. A full meeting of all senior staff at noon. Be there.' He put his hand on her shoulder in a painful grip, adding, 'If you're not there, I'm quite prepared to come and fetch you. Don't think you can escape from me, Lexi Brooke.' He turned to James, ushering him into the waiting car. As he swung his athletic frame after him, Lexi heard him say, 'And you, cousin, have a heck of a lot of explaining to do.'

Lexi shivered, and pulled her jacket round her. It was going to be a cold day.

Anya was unperturbed by her friend's sudden reappearance in the flat. She was well accustomed to Lexi's unexpected comings and goings. They snatched a quick breakfast together whilst Lexi brought her up to date. Anya sipped her coffee thoughtfully, eyes frankly speculative, watching the animation and sparkle in Lexi's eyes, as she declared how much she disliked Cade Chamberlyane.

'Looks to me as though you've met your match at last, and,' she added, 'in spite of what you say, you paint a very attractive picture of him.'

'He's a brute.' Lexi wasn't prepared to reveal, or even examine, her true feelings for Cade. To admit to them would imply a loss of control, and she hated that. Somehow, whilst she was Hetty Smythe, it had been easier. Now there was no-one to hide behind, she had to erect a wall of defence around her own persona. She knew, only too well, how easily she could succumb to the electric magnetism of her boss. 'I'll shower and change, and then I've got to go, Anya. Goodness knows when I'll see you again. Sir will probably arrange dormitory accommodation for us all until we've done what's required. I'll be under house arrest, in all probability, over the week-end. Fortunately, there's nothing on that I can't cancel. Though I must admit, I'm sorely tempted.'

Anya laughed, but forebore to comment that, for someone who professed to hate her employer, Lexi looked remarkably lit up by the prospect of being quartered with him for the duration.

It had already happened at the security gate — and at Reception. No-one recognised her. Madeleine Honeywell, too, looked up as Lexi walked into the office, then, after a sidelong glance at her diary, said rather frostily, 'Do you have an appointment? Reception didn't tell me . . .'

'Lexi — Lexi Brooke. Mr Chamberlayne's PA started on Monday. We've been to San Diego,' she added rather unnecessarily.

'Lexi!' Madeleine gasped. 'But . . . she . . . you . . . ' She peered more closely at the tall girl whose dark thick hair was already returning to its natural dark gold, and whose wide grey-green eyes were unconcealed by contact lenses. The plain sensible suit had been replaced by a short, fitted skirt and cream silk shirt. High heels showed off her lovely legs.

Lexi was stating her own personality — there was no longer any point in concealment. She looked ruefully at Mrs Honeywell, feeling guilty. 'It's a long story. I'm sorry.'

'You sound like the woman I met Friday, but you don't look much like her. What on earth's happened?'

Lexi was released from explanations by an impatient buzz on the intercom. Cade's voice was briskly decisive. 'Madeleine, the files on Lennox, there seems to be one missing. Prices of their last year's range.'

'I'll check — oh — and Lexi's here. Do you want her in with you?'

'Where else? What's she hanging about for? We don't have much time. Tell her to get in here, and stop all calls until after the meeting.' The click at the other end was impatient.

Madeleine raised her eyebrows. 'He's been like that all morning. I don't look forward to the rest of the day. Better get going — and — best of luck! By the way,' she smiled warmly, 'don't bother to explain, but you look great!'

Lexi smiled back appreciative thanks, swallowed hard, and knocked on Cade's door.

★ ★ ★

By the time the meeting was due, Lexi had been fully briefed on the situation. The launch of Cosmogems' new range had been, until now, set for the next Friday. The theme, so carefully researched and put together, was to be skin care, rather than totally cosmetic. The products were to be high quality, top of the range, the logo stressing health. Lennox, a large rival company, had stressed exactly those factors, even to the colour of the packaging — theirs being only slighty deeper in tone. If Cosmogems went ahead with their launch, it would look like a copy cat operation — the impact pre-empted. The only item on the agenda of the noon meeting was what action to take.

Cade had taken her swiftly through all the costings and procedures of launching a new range. She learned fast and, as always when working with him, she felt her brain was more alive, more stimulated, zinging with ideas, buzzing with questions. She found it exhilarating, and it seemed that, in working together, they were in total harmony, with no hint of suspicion or animosity, although she knew full well that that could return at any moment.

★ ★ ★

Madeleine brought in a tray of coffee and sandwiches at half past eleven. They'd been working for two hours. 'Half an hour to go. I thought you'd want to carry on, but you must have something to eat. You didn't have breakfast, I'm sure.'

Cade smiled at his secretary, and Lexi again noticed the warmth of his look. Madeleine Honeywell. Divorced? Widowed? A little old for Cade — maybe fortyish. Perhaps not. Stop it, she chided herself, what's it got to do with you? Yet she couldn't stop the return of that rib sticking pain at the thought of Cade and his secretary! Impossible. Yet there had to be a girlfriend somewhere.

'Lexi?' Madeleine looked at her enquiringly. 'Coffee?'

She started. 'Please — wonderful.'

'Cade, you're overworking Lexi. No sleep — she'll keel over at this rate.'

'No chance. There's too much to do.

121

Don't worry, Maddy, she's a tough nut!'

Lexi flushed at the unflattering description. 'Don't worry, Madeleine. Really. There's a lot to know, but I'm managing fine.'

'Well, don't overdo it, Cade.'

His secretary looked severe, and Cade touched her arm. 'Don't worry. And thanks for the food — and coffee. See you at the meeting.' As she went out, he turned back to Lexi. 'You should have a clear picture now. You'll need to adopt a high profile at the meeting, and I'll want your assessment report afterwards. It'll be useful for me to have a fresh eye looking at what goes on. Any problems?'

Lexi shook her head. 'No.' She spoke confidently, but inwardly felt a small tremor. 'High profile'! At her first meeting? She wondered how that would go down with Cosmogems' executives.

'Right, let's go.' Cade shuffled some papers into his briefcase and stood up.

Lexi followed him to the door. Courteously, he made to open it, pausing to look at her, the amber prominent in his eyes as his stare raked her from shining hair to elegant shoe. 'Well, well,' he said softly, the hard dynamic manner cloaked momentarily, 'who would have thought it? If it was James who fouled the whole thing up, that'll be another score to settle with him.'

Lexi felt heat rise in her at his caressing tone. He was very close, one hand across her body, reaching for the door handle. She shrank away, but the silkiness of his next words furnaced through her.

'I mean the opportunity I might have missed — to show you the gems — the night sky of the Mexican desert.' He opened the door and, with shaking legs, Lexi preceded him into the outer office.

There was nothing soft about Cade during the next hour. Lexi wondered if she'd dreamed those quietly murmured words, imagined that comprehensive look. The Cade who chaired the meeting of Cosmogems' senior staff was all ice, authority, and ruthless determination. Every chair at the long table but two was filled when they arrived. Lexi noted the ratio of women to men was about fifty fifty — about a dozen in all.

He drew out the chair next to his, and motioned her to sit. 'Lexi Brooke, my new PA Lexi — James and Bella, I think you've met. The others . . . ' He went around the table — Finance, Marketing, Design, Personnel — all the usual company divisions. Polite nods greeted her; closed expressions, biding time, waiting for Cade's direction, waiting to assess Lexi's own performance. James hardly looked at her. Bella's gasp of astonishment at her appearance was followed by a hard, narrow-eyed stare. No doubt of the hostility there, Lexi registered. At least Madeleine, preparing to take notes on the other side of Cade, gave her a wide encouraging smile.

'Let's get down to it.' Cade was

sharp. 'For the present, I'm not prepared to discuss the hows and whys of what happened to allow our chief competitors to get details of our new range, and to pre-empt us by an impossibly embarrassing short week. It looks pretty calculated to me. Make no mistake, I'm going to get to the bottom of it. Once this fiasco's been sorted out, I'm going to find out what — or who — is trying to make darned sure Cosmogems keeps falling flat on its face lately. When I do find out . . . ' His gaze swept the room, eyes fractionally pausing on each face, he finished with quiet, but deadly emphasis . . . 'Heaven help him — or her!'

There was total silence — no-one stirred or moved a muscle. Lexi held her breath, trying to read beyond the shuttered, downcast expressions.

It was Cade who broke the tension. 'What we have to do now,' he spoke more matter of factly, 'is find a way out of this. Cancel — or postpone. I'll take your views — then decide.'

A buzz went round the room — something positive to do. Lexi felt the relief. Someone was off the hook — for the moment!

Discussion was free-ranging and democratic. Cade was informal, but decisive. Opinon seemed split down the middle in favour of postponement. After about half an hour, Cade turned to Lexi who, so far, had said nothing. 'Your view please.'

A surge of adrenaline shot through her. Now was the time to play her Career Woman role. She smiled at Cade. 'Thanks. I'd like to suggest something, if I may. I think all the arguments given are valid. Postponement lets Lennox gain ground in the market. Cancellation admits defeat. Why not keep the same launch date, make the same arrangements, but a different range? A new theme.'

'Such as?' Cade asked. The meeting was very quiet. 'Do you have an idea?'

'Of course, otherwise I wouldn't have suggested it.' Her tone challenged him, and she saw a tiny pulse beat in his throat. Bella was scowling a black, familiar Chamberlayne scowl. Lexi had seen the same look in Cade's face. 'I haven't had time to work out details, and I'm not sure about the timing. A week's not long.'

'An understatement. It's ridiculous.' Bella snapped across the table.

Cade out-scowled his niece. 'Let her finish.'

Bella threw him a malevolent look, and the tension level in the room rose perceptibly.

Lexi hurriedly continued. 'I thought we could link cosmetics to jewellery. Enhance the normal range — we've lots of stock — by linking it with specific gems: for instance, moisturiser with diamonds, diamond drops, earrings maybe, or pearls; skin freshener with crystals; colours, lipsticks, for example, with gem colours, rubies and garnets; eye colourings with sapphires, or jade. I know it's a different concept from the original, but it would be an attempt to popularise Cosmogems, and broaden the appeal. Come down market a little — catch the public imagination. The orginal skin care concept could be a follow up.' She paused to assess reaction. Several faces looked interested — there were nods of approval. She noted that the Head of Design, Peter Roberts, had started to doodle — pictures of gems.

He looked up. 'I like it. It's different.'

'We can't revamp at this stage,' Mike Simmonds, finance director, put in.

'I'm not suggesting a revamp. Shelve your original idea for a month or so. Go all out on this one as a pre-run. Surely it's only a matter of design and repackaging. Publicity.' She looked at Bella, who was responsible for advertising through her editorial section.

'It's got great possibilities,' Peter Roberts enthused.

Lexi smiled directly at him. He seemed a likely ally.

'Absolute nonsense,' Bella stormed in. 'Impossible in the time, and it would do Cosmogems' image no good whatso-ever. We don't have to go down market. We never have done.'

'Perhaps now is the time you should,' Lexi returned quietly.

Bella spat fury. 'What can you possibly know about Cosmogems? You've not been here five minutes! You can't run a new campaign in a week. It's stupid and naive. Shows how little business experience you have.'

'Bella! That's enough. Lexi has an equal voice here. And there's no need to be rude.'

His niece's face suffused with rage. She half rose in her seat, but James put out a restraining hand, and she subsided, directing a basilisk stare at Lexi.

'I don't think it's possible to fix it up in a week.' Jayne, elegantly sleek, in charge of the jewellery division, was doubtful.

'Why not? Cade asked. 'We're all tooled up. The products are there. As Lexi says, it's all a question of

129

packaging, copywriting and teamwork.'

'A week?' Another voice of disbelief.

There was a pause. Everyone's attention was on Cade. He sat back in his chair, relaxed and easy, long legs splayed out in front of him. He brought his finger tips together and spoke deliberately, without the snap and crackle of the early part of the meeting. 'This is a crisis for Cosmogems. We've had a series lately! If word gets out as planned, apparently a copy cat operation, wouldn't do us much good. I think Lexi's got something. I also think it's possible. We've got all the resources, equipment, and personnel. All it would take is time — and dedication. If a team was to work non-stop from now, through the week-end, to Friday, it could be done. I know proper publicity will be impossible, Bella, but there are ways and means. You're more than capable of coming up with something brilliant.' He glanced at his watch. 'But I do mean non stop — starting now. I'm all for it — that's what we'll do.

Any objections?' Now he sat forward, hands on the edge of the table, eyes daring anyone to dissent.

Bella defiantly raised her hand — it was the only one.

'Right.' Cade stood up. 'James, Bella, Jayne, Mike, Pete, Lexi — you're the nucleus. Call on any division for help — you're to be given top priority. Lexi — keep me well in the picture. This is your project. The others,' he looked directly at Bella, 'will back her completely.'

Bella tossed her head, mutiny expressed in every line of her body. Lexi's spirit quailed at the thought of working with her, but she would be a vital cog in the machine. Cade had put her firmly in her place, but Bella didn't look the biddable sort. Lexi knew it wouldn't be an easy ride. A fine start to her six months sentence!

As the meeting broke up, Cade spoke to James. 'Start the ball rolling. You can make it easy for Lexi — show her the short cuts.'

The team nucleus stayed behind, forming a small knot. Pete held out his hand. 'Welcome, Lexi Brooke. I think this'll be fun.' The others added their greetings — only Bella remaining obstinately aloof.

Cade picked up his briefcase, and nodded at Madeleine to follow him. 'Good luck, team. I'll keep in touch.' His eyes rested on Lexi. In their green depths was a look of — something indefinable. A look specially for her. It turned her stomach to water.

6

By the following Tuesday, Lexi was convinced that six months in Dartmoor would have been preferable to her present work load. She was already punch drunk with new information; absorbing new techniques, designing and redesigning, editing and re-editing. They'd all worked through Friday until midnight, re-assembling early on Saturday in a strangely ghostly and silent building. Until they had hammered out the format of the new approach, the factory and laboratory were closed as usual at the week-end.

Late Saturday, she was beginning to think she'd taken on an impossible task; by Sunday evening, she was ready to give in, and on Monday, bleary eyed and yawning, she went into Cade's office. He was at a computer, one of several on a work top at one end of the office, absorbed by the figures on the V.D.U. He had his back to her, and she could see his intense concentration from the tight set of his shoulders and the taut, rigidness of his whole body.

'Cade.' She spoke tentatively.

He spun round in the swivel chair, a frown on his face. 'Lexi — what's the problem? Why aren't you on the project? Is there anything wrong?'

Everything, she thought grimly. I'm exhausted, your niece is a fiend incarnate, James is useless, and you haven't been near the place all week-end. That, she particularly resented. All that talk about round the clock dedication — apparently it didn't apply to the Managing Director! They were working a fifteen hour day whilst Cade, seemingly, swanned off for the week-end. She'd conscientiously sent him a daily progress report, and his response had been total silence.

'Well?' he said impatiently, his eyes sliding round to the screen.

'You haven't been near the project.

We've been worked flat out — all week-end.' Lexi hadn't meant to say that, and she was horrified to catch the petulant whine in her voice.

Cade looked surprised. 'I know, it's all in your report. It seems to be going very well.'

Lexi longed to ask 'and where were you at the week-end?' Instead, she said crossly, 'It's an impossible task. I was wrong. We can't possibly be ready by Friday.'

'Why not?'

She opened her mouth, but thought better of it. What was the use? Without Bella on the project, it may have been possible. James, at least, didn't try to thwart everything she was trying to do. He wasn't positively helpful, but James she could deal with, and the others were co-operative, their enthusiasm growing daily. 'There's just not enough time,' she said lamely.

'Nonsense. Have some coffee. Maddy's just brought some in — strong and black. Here.' He poured her a cup from the jug on the table, and stood over her, his hands resting lightly on his hips. 'Pete's wild about the whole thing. You've impressed him, at least.'

'You've spoken to him?' Lexi was surprised. Pete had been matching her hour by hour on the project. She couldn't see how he'd found the time to see Cade.

'I told you, Lexi.' His voice held a familiar note of threat. 'You're on trial. You're here for a reason. If you are part of a conspiracy, at least I'm getting good value from you.'

She sprang up to face him. 'You can't still think I'm some sort of industrial spy. Why would I be working so hard?'

Cade shrugged. 'A perfect cover? And there's always a next time.'

'You're just using me.' Her voice was high.

'Sure. All's fair in love, war, and business. You can't chicken out now!' He swivelled back to his computer, his back towards her again.

Rage and tiredness overwhelming her

for a few moments, made her feel dizzy. She clenched her fists, and fought for control. There was nothing she could do except carry on regardless and hope that she could stand the difficult coming months at Cosmogems.

In fact, her encounter with Cade stiffened her resolve. With renewed energy, she flung herself into the project, anxious to succeed, to finish it, then, however long a shot it was, try to find out for herself what was happening to Cosmogems.

From then on, the launch of 'Crystal Line' was assured. Lexi saw it as a personal gauntlet flung down by Cade. She played the role of a bossy virago, galvanising James, and confronting Bella head on, telling her in no uncertain terms that, unless she co-operated fully, Cade would be told, she'd be off the project, and one of her junior staff put on it instead. At first, Bella blustered, threw a haughty tantrum, accused Lexi of all manner of things, but finally caved in with a very bad grace, and started to be constructive. Lexi would have preferred her to be out of the way for comfort, but from the point of view of Crystal Line's success, she was a decided asset. Her advertising copy was brilliant, she had a sharp mind, and Lexi had to admire her talent and expertise with words and slogans. She was in no doubt that Bella had declared a very temporary truce, and that the knives would be out immediately the launch was over. Bella would always be her enemy, and six months could seem a lifetime — but afterwards, Lexi could put several countries between herself and the entire Chamberlayne set-up. The sudden pain at the thought of that prospect was dull and hollow — different from the sharp stabs of inexplicable jealousy she'd felt at the thought of Cade and whoever was his current girlfriend. He must have lots of choice — Cosmogems bristled with wonderfully elegant, svelte women, from receptionists to models. One of the models they were using for the cosmetic launch talked ceaselessly of Cade, and hinted that they were more than 'good friends' so that Lexi had another stilletto stab to contend with.

'All wishful thinking,' Pete had said one day, bored with the incessant chatter. 'Cade's not interested in anyone connected with Cosmogems. He learned that lesson years ago. Once bitten . . . '

'What?'

But Pete was immersed in a new set of drawings. 'Now — what about this satin white, gold embossed pack, for the moisturiser.'

Lexi was left to surmise what she would from that tantalising titbit!

* * *

By Thursday night they congratulated each other that they'd made it. A new range of basic cosmetics was ready. Each product was accompanied by a specially designed piece of costume jewellery. Lexi's favourite was a necklace and bracelet of garnets, rubies and moonstone gems, reflecting a new range of lipstick shades. She, herself, could see all the hallmarks of a rushed campaign, but they'd joined the seams cleverly, and she didn't think it would show. It was brash, exciting, and modern, and she was sure, if nothing went wrong on the Friday launch, it would prove to be a popular success.

All they had to do was set up the exhibition at the Conference Centre in the city. The whole machinery; celebrity stars, champagne, catering — had been laid on months ago for the original launch. Bella's publicity, finally, had been splendid and blanket mail slots to all appropriate buyers, and saturation peak time TV advertisements for a week. How Bella had fixed that at such short notice, Lexi hadn't enquired.

The five o'clock Friday deadline was reached with only minutes to spare, and then, as far as Lexi was concerned, the whole venture was on automatic. The atmosphere began to buzz as people arrived, champagne circulated, and the models prepared to perform.

Pete stood next to her as the audience settled. 'Have a glass yourself,' he said, 'you deserve it.'

Automatically, she took the wine from him. 'Where's Cade? Surely he's going to be here.'

'He's probably decided to make an entrance. He was here for a few minutes earlier in the day. He seems satisfied.'

'That's a relief!' Lexi couldn't keep the sarcasm out of her voice.

Pete looked at her in surprise, then nudged her. 'Here he is. What did I tell you — and wowee — look who he's got with him.'

The man and woman poised at the entrance were a magnificent advertisement for charisma and glamour. Cade's dark trousers and white dinner jacket highlighted his magnetic masculinity, and complemented the glittering, black and white sequinned mini dress worn by the woman at his side. Her arm was tucked proprietorially in his, and Lexi recognised her. She was the same woman who had hung on his arm in the convention ballroom in San Diego! This had to be his current girlfriend!

'Who is she?' She had to ask, although it gave her no pleasure to hear Pete tell her that she was the daughter of a fabulously wealthy tycoon, and already making a fortune in her own right as a top model.

'Trust Cade to pick the best of the bunch,' Pete spoke to the empty air. Lexi had gone.

She felt no compunction in returning to the flat. Selling the 'Crystal Line' idea was up to Cade, James, the models, and, ultimately, the entire Sales Section. After her efforts of the past week, she didn't feel that her legs would carry her through two hours or more of cocktail chat and sales pressure hype. All she wanted was a hot bath, and a very long sleep — a sleep which she hoped would consign to oblivion the sight of Cade smiling down at his glamorous partner.

Instead, it kept her awake. Anya was away for the week-end, the flat was quiet, but Lexi's racing thoughts refused to settle. She had to get away from Cosmogems! Maybe if the launch was successful, and nothing else bad happened, he'd release her from her contract. In the small hours of the night, her own resolve to try and find out if there was a conspiracy against the firm looked ridiculous. The only speck of evidence was the disk she'd found in Cade's briefcase in San Diego. That might lead somewhere. Cade had burst in before she could print out the information, but she remembered it vividly, and why it had worried her. The screen had shown sets of figures costing Cosmogems entire cosmetic range. But the figures bore no comparison to the ones Cade had given her to study. His showed competitive prices across the range, well in line, and often below their current competitors. The figures on the disk showed prices a uniform ten per cent above competitors. No wonder orders were falling if these were the prices circulated. Lexi couldn't believe that Cade wouldn't be aware of the discrepancies — he had the disk in his case. Yet she was very much aware that Cade's management style was to delegate. She'd seen a prime example of that with 'Crystal Line' — he'd left it entirely to her. So, if he hadn't seen the disk! If someone was tampering with current price lists, it seemed a very risky thing to do. Whoever it was must be banking on Cade's complete ignorance of anything to do with Sales! Finally she gave up. There was nothing she could do until Monday.

★   ★   ★

It seemed only two minutes later that she was dragged out of a deep and dreamless sleep by her bedside phone ringing. Fumbling for the receiver, her brain was fogged with sleep. 'Mmmm,' was all she could muster.

'Lexi.' His voice was very wide awake. Unmistakable. 'Do you realise it's midday? You're still in bed? Why did you rush away from the launch last night?' The questions were quick fire — staccato.

She sat up, pushing her hair away from her face. How easily he could make her defensively resentful. 'I'd finished my part in the project. What was left was selling and public relations. That was your part of it.'

'Anything I have to do includes you. Didn't you want to see how it went?'

'I expect you'll tell me — especially if it wasn't successful.' She didn't apologise for being in bed. She reckoned Cosmogems owed her a few hours sleep, and it was Saturday. There was silence at the other end of the line. Not like Cade. She cleared her throat.

The silence broke. 'Have dinner with me tonight.' It was more a command than an invitation.

'What for?' Lexi was bewildered.

The deep, sensual laugh was confident. 'Because I'd like you to, and I think you'd like it, too. I'll pick you up at eight o'clock.'

'Er — I may not be free.'

'Nothing you can't get out of. You can go back to sleep now.'

She stared at the phone for a long time, yawned prodigiously, repressed a shiver of excitement, stuck her head under the pillow, did as she was told, and went back to sleep.

* * *

A few hours later, feeling her own self again, she was out jogging, trying to compensate for the previous week's lack of exercise. Tensions eased away from her, as her long stride took her round her local park.

Her natural optimism and ebullience resurfaced. All that business with the figures seemed ludicrous in the light of day. All she had to do was convince Cade of her own innocence. He was

146

perfectly capable of carrying out his own investigations. She didn't want to be involved. She wondered about the dinner invitation — maybe it was an excuse for further inquisition into her personal life. She hesitated over what to wear. Cade was obviously used to the high life, but a perverse sense of obstinacy dictated her choice of black velvet trousers and a semi-casual, gold coloured top. She wasn't going to dress up, although the extra high heels were a subconscious defence against Cade's dominating figure. Even so, when she answered the door to him, precisely at eight, she still had to tilt her head back to look into his eyes.

He was casually dressed, dark shirt open necked, a soft, leather jacket sitting easily on his broad shoulders. It was the first time Lexi had seen him without a suit. He looked younger, but her heart wrenched when he smiled at her, a smile purely for her, warm and wide, the mouth promising in its curve, a hint of sensuality and passion. She steeled herself. It wasn't for her, and she wondered again why he was wasting a Saturday evening on her.

A taxi was waiting in the street.

'I want to enjoy some wine with you,' Cade explained. 'This way I can relax. Don't look so suspicious, Lexi, you're not at work now.'

'I've practically forgotten what it's like not to be at work lately — and you're the suspicious one, remember.'

His mouth was taut, but he replied lightly. 'I thought we might enjoy this evening. You've worked very hard. I appreciate that.'

It sounded like an incentive bonus, and Lexi wondered if the rest of the team were to be wined and dined — probably all meet up in a few minutes for a planning and analysis meeting, she thought wryly, prepared for anything where Cade was concerned.

But the evening was for her alone and Cade set out to entertain and charm to please and flatter. He set the scene in a small, unpretentious restaurant where he was obviously well known. The service was discreet, the food and wine excellent, but Lexi was hardly aware of what she ate. His presence glowed around her, his eyes held hers, he touched her fingers as they chose the wine, and she felt the same lethargy as in San Diego, when he'd massaged her tense muscles. She tried to fight it, but decided to bow to the inevitable, and flow with the evening. After all, it was only a dinner!

'Crystal Line will be a great success. You did a superb job. Congratulations!' He lifted his glass to hers. 'This wine matches your hair — deep gold.' He touched the thick waves at her neck and laid his fingers at the base of her throat. 'Honey dark dangerous coils,' he murmured caressingly, immediately followed by a brisk, 'lots of interest last night. Bella's done a great job for the Sunday papers. I wouldn't be surprised to see an upturn in share prices on Monday.'

Lexi couldn't help asking, 'Do you

think — whatever's going on — is over now?'

'Don't let's discuss it tonight. Time — or you — will tell,' he said enigmatically, and changed the subject. 'How did you get on with Bella? She can be a bit difficult.'

Lexi spluttered into her wine. 'What an understatement — she's a . . . ' She saw Cade's face, and paused. 'A little trying.' But her eyes clouded as she remembered Bella's barbs and slights through the week. 'She seems to have a chip on her shoulder about something.'

'Bella's the only child of my eldest brother, Charles, and his wife, both dead now. They had her very late in life, probably over indulged her. She can be headstrong, but she's going through a bad patch — a difficult divorce. I'm executor of her parents' estate. She's a little impatient to get at the money, which is in trust. As a trustee, I handle her affairs, and she resents that. She'd also like a lot more power and say in the running of Cosmogems. She was none too pleased when I turned down her idea for a magazine.'

'You did turn it down then?'

'Of course — you were absolutely right, particulary now, at this point in the company's history. I'm only telling you this to explain Bella. She's angry at me, not you, except by connection.'

Lexi wasn't too sure he was right, but kept her own counsel.

'It's always been company policy to employ family — right back to great grandfather's day. His motto was 'belief in the family is belief in self'.

'Doesn't it lead to problems sometimes? Conflicts — rivalries?'

Cade shrugged. 'It's worked well so far. Jabez Chamberlayne was an idealist as well as a practical man. The family ideal was important to him, and is to all of us. Anyone who speaks against a Chamberlayne, speaks against us all.'

'Sounds feudal to me, but the story of Jabez and his Mexican bride is really romantic.'

Cade laughed, and picked up her hand, turning it palm upwards. 'That old legend! If you believe that, you'll believe I can read your hand!'

'It's not true then — Jabez falling in love with the daughter of a Mexican peasant, who made him work seven years on his land before he'd allow the marriage?'

'I doubt it. Jabez was very canny. It made a good romantic story as part of Gemco's early publicity. From what I gather from Jabez, it's more likely he made use of his peasant father-in-law's mineral rights to mine his land for silver, and with the proceeds set up his business in England. You're a romantic, Lexi. I'd never have thought it. Maybe I need to change the Miss Prim version of you I still can't help clinging on to. I should look for that wild cat underneath the artificial exterior. I don't think that was acting.'

He touched his lips to her fingers, and a tremor ran through her. Hastily, she pulled her hand away and picked up her wine glass. 'This Burgundy's pretty good, too,' she said over-brightly.

Cade laughed, and drank from his glass, his eyes on her lips. 'So it is,' he agreed gravely. Let's see if it compliments the pheasant as much as that top flatters your figure.'

His mood was so amiable and relaxed, Lexi was tempted to tell him about the disk, and its odd costings, but she was loth to spoil the atmosphere, and — she needed to find the tape. Cade would accuse her of imagining the whole thing, or worse, inventing it.

The magic evening went on. After dinner they moved on to a night club and danced, Lexi dangerously aware of her melting feelings towards him. Too much charm, wine and music, she surmised, as he finally called a taxi and took her back to the flat.

'Coffee?' he said softly. His lips were so close to her ear, every nerve end screamed for him to come closer.

'It's — rather late.'

'Another time.' He took her in his

153

arms and kissed her, a sweet unde-
manding kiss, as one to a good friend
and comrade after a pleasant time spent
together. There was no trace of the
angry passion she'd experienced in her
bedroom at the Arlington Plaza in San
Diego. 'Thanks, Lexi. For Crystal Line.'
He held the taxi, walked her up the
stairs to the door of the flat, touched
her cheek with his lips, and was gone.

She heard the engine rev as the taxi
moved away, a hollow sense of anti-
climax descending as she opened the
front door. It occurred to her that she
didn't even know where he lived — or
who with? The dinner had been a
'thanks' from employer to employee,
and Cade was such a potent male
animal it was instinctive for him to flirt
with any woman he took out — for
whatever reason.

7

'Crystal Line' was set to be a commercial and popular success, the latter helped by Bella's romantically appealing pre-launch blurb about the company's family history. She'd retold the story of Jabez, the patriarch, his young Mexican wife, Maria, his sister, Elizabeth, with her herbs and potions. It hit the right note. Family solidarity, business enterprise, natural products, Mexican silver. Cosmogems was on to a winner. The trickle of advance orders promised to become a flood as the days went on. The company had a high news profile, with sales graphs beginning an upward trend.

Since taking her out to dinner, Cade had been brisk and businesslike. He delegated more and more of his routine work to her, demanding long hours of intense concentration. There was no time to even think of the disk. Cosmogems' fortunes seemed to be on the ascendant, and she fervently hoped that Cade's pet theory about her involvement in its troubles would be knocked on the head with Crystal Line's success.

Lexi found it increasingly difficult to work closely with Cade. He was far too disturbing to her emotions, and his apparent indifference to her fuelled her nervous edginess when he was around. Only when they were both totally absorbed in some abstruse piece of company analysis did she find some ease, so that when their minds were actively engaged, she was able to forget her physical reactions to his potent attraction.

During the second week, following the launch of Crystal Line, Cade called her into his office to go over some follow up reports from his skin care speech at the San Diego Convention. 'The message is finally getting through. It looks as if some of the other people at the Convention agree with me: more research in skin diseases and allergies — we need funds, donations to hospitals, grants to Medical Schools. I've had an invitation to set up a committee to look into it.' He raked a hand through his usually immaculately groomed hair, the dark curls springing in all directions. He took off his jacket, tossing it carelessly onto a chair, loosened his tie, and swivelled round in his big chair. He looked ten years younger, fired with crusading zeal, Cosmogems' troubles forgotten for the moment.

'You really like this part of your work, don't you?' Lexi picked up the files he'd pushed towards her, and made to take them into her office.

'No — work in here, it'll be quicker if we go through these together. I want the date on this computer.' He leaned back. 'Yes, I do enjoy this part. Sometimes I'm tempted to turn cosmetics and jewellery entirely over to James, and get on with this.' He tapped the papers on his desk. 'Maybe when Cosmogems is solid again.'

'Things are going well then? No more problems?' she ventured tentatively.

'No. Should there be?' The suspicious frown was back.

Lexi sighed. 'Cade, I know you still suspect me. It's absolute nonsense. And why should trouble come from inside the Company? Couldn't the problems come from outside competitors — rival firms?

His laugh wasn't pretty. 'Of course it's rival companies — but those rival companies, or company, have had information that only someone working here would have — and someone who knows our security inside out. No — there've been too many coincidences, too many leakages and rumours — all designed to damage us. Crystal Line's the only good thing to happen lately, and that's because you rushed it through so fast — no-one had the chance to sabotage it. Thanks again.'

His smile hinted of his awareness of her as a woman.

I can't stand it, she thought, her brain flashing a warning. 'Cade,' she pleaded urgently, 'release me from my contract — please!'

Green eyes flashed danger, ominous storm clouds chased out the previous warmth. He banged his hands down on the desk. 'No,' he rasped, 'you're staying. Six months! You go when I say, not a moment before.' He picked up his jacket. 'I've got an appointment. You finish up here. I want an abstract of all this before you leave. I'll pick it up in the morning, and take it on the plane with me.' With a furious backward glance, he stormed out of the office, his jacket hooked over his shoulder by one finger, his tie still awry.

'Cade!'

Madeleine jumped up as he passed her office, but he ignored her, striding at speed towards the lifts.

'Well! What caused that?' she asked as Lexi came out of the office.

'I — I just asked him to terminate my contract . . . '

'Why?'

The question was sharp, and Lexi shot Cade's secretary a puzzled look. Was she getting paranoid, or was there something odd about Mrs Honeywell's reaction.

'You've made such a difference to Cade — his work, I mean. You've taken off the pressure, and then Crystal Line, it'd be a shame if you left.'

She sounded genuine, but Lexi wasn't sure of anything any more. Cade's change of mood was bewildering, and she hated the way her will seemed to be slipping out of control. Better to leave Cosmogems — let Cade sue her! Rather that than the slow burning torture of having to be with him and his suspicions.

Madeleine was putting on her coat. 'Aren't you going home, Lexi? It's late already.'

'No. I've still some stuff to finish. I'll be quite late.'

'Cade works you too hard. He forgets everyone doesn't have his energy.'

'Oh, I'm a tough nut,' Lexi said ruefully, 'I'll survive.'

'I'm sure you will,' Mrs Honeywell said as she left the office.

* * *

Some hours later, with a weary sigh, Lexi rubbed her eyes and switched off the computer. All Cade's data on the San Diego Conference was up to date, in one long abstract. 'Beautifully presented.' She clapped her hand to her mouth. Her words, spoken out loud, echoed round the room. It was late. The Security Officers had been on their rounds twice already. It was eerie in the deserted building. Time to go home. She switched off the light by the door, and froze. There were footsteps outside, voices raised in argument. She put her hand on the door, then stopped. The footsteps and voices went into Mrs Honeywell's office, but that door was open and she could hear every word. She recognised the two voices.

'I'm worried, and Mike's getting edgy. Cade's bound to find out soon. He's on to finance next week. It'll never work.'

James' voice was sharply and unmistakeably answered by Bella's. 'Don't be wimpish. He never bothers with mundane details, especially now he's got his precious Ms Brooke doing his donkey work. She won't spot it, Cade's given her too much to do — fortunately. Just keep your nerve. Anyway, even if he finds out, he'd never do anything. We're family.'

'I wouldn't count on it.' James' voice sank to a murmur.

Lexi heard drawers being opened, rustlings, bleeps and taps, at the computer keyboard. She held her breath.

'And tampering about with a few figures isn't going to bring Cosmogems tumbling.' James' voice was faintly querulous.

'Just hang in there, Uncle James. It's a small beginning, but I'm building up for the big one — very soon. If that doesn't work, nothing will. We'll soon have you as Managing Director. We're long overdue for a change.'

'What are you up to now?' James' anxiety was palpable.

'Best you don't know. Just leave it to me — I have my contacts. You'd be surprised how much damage a few whispers can do. I'm off to New York with Cade in the morning. I'll be away in the clear when the storm breaks.'

'Bella, you promised — nothing dramatic, or dangerous. No harm to Cade — or to Cosmogems. Otherwise . . .'

' . . . otherwise you wouldn't have joined Mike and I in our little scheme, would you Uncle? Don't worry. Cosmogems will forge ahead with such a dynamic trio in charge, instead of my malevolent, despotic Uncle Cade?' She spat out the name angrily, and Lexi felt sick at the depth of hatred in her voice.

At last, she heard them go — lights snapped off, and then the distant whine of the lift descending. She leaned weakly against the door. Cade need look no further than his own backyard. It was incredible — and dangerous! They must be mad! Whatever scheme they cooked up wasn't going to fool Cade for long. In any case, she'd have to tell him herself what she'd heard. She locked Cade's door and went into the outer office, just as the lights snapped on again. Bella stood framed in the doorway.

'You,' she gasped as Lexi moved forward. 'Why are you here?'

'Working late,' Lexi replied, far more calmly than she felt. 'And you?'

Bella's mouth was a hard line, her black eyes menacing. 'How long have you been here? Didn't you hear James and I — we were — checking some figures — on Crystal Line — for the press. I left my car keys on the desk.'

'No.' Lexi crossed her fingers. 'I was busy. Cade left me a stack of work to be steamed through before he leaves in the morning. No time to look up at all.' She stepped into Madeleine's office. 'Are these your keys?'

Bella took them from her, eyes narrowing. 'Remember, Miss Brooks, this is a family business. Outsiders have little credibility where family members are concerned. You'd never be believed.' It was hardly an oblique warning.

Lexi's anger rose. 'I'm well aware of the nature of Cosmogems set up.'

Bella stared at her coldly, then turned on her heels and left. Lexi followed more slowly — she had no wish to share the lift with Bella Weston!

★ ★ ★

The next morning, her abstract had gone. Cade must have been in early. The New York trip had been set up weeks ago. He and Bella were to investigate the possibility of setting up a subsidiary of Cosmogems in the States. Just up Bella's street, Lexi thought,

165

wishing she would stay there for good!

She'd been given a brief reprieve, but her nerves jangled at the thought of telling Cade what she'd overheard. She tried desperately hard to forget both Cade and Cosmogems, but his image remained obstinately in her head, and her brain raced around all the possibilities of Bella's machinations. She had an uneasy feeling that something was going to erupt.

In the event, it was nothing particularly dramatic — at first. Cosmogems shares had been edging upwards as a result of Crystal Line's success, but as trading got under way on Monday, they shot to a new high. Rumours began to circulate that Lennox, their rival company, had made a takeover bid which was under consideration by Cosmogems board. James immediately issued an ambiguous denial which was taken as an evasion. Lennox management was non-committal. A merchant bank professed interest, 'if Cosmogems was up for sale', and shares rose even higher.

A furious Cade called from New York, commanding James to scotch all the rumours. News of Cade's vehemence added fuel to the fire of rumour and counter rumour and, by the end of the day, no-one could sort out fact from fiction. The Cosmogems building buzzed with speculation, and everyone waited on tenterhooks for Cade's return.

Stock market activity didn't often harm sales — merely created uncertainty, with reverberations in the financial world, but a feature on Tuesday in a popular tabloid would harm sales, and certainly would dent the 'clean cut' ecologically sound image Cade had tried to build up.

'Crystal Line, Crystal Clear? Muddy Waters at Cosmogems!' The bold headline prefaced a report alleging that a secret and anonymous laboratory, Cosmogems was developing a new skin product, based on animal testing. The article purported to expose the 'pious hypocrisy' of Cosmogems Managing

Director, Cade Chamberlayne, who posed as 'apostle of the pure and natural'.

The double-spread feature raised the whole question of experiments on animals once again, listing companies with clean records, and citing those whose methods were still questionable. There was a fuzzy long shot of a low, substantially built brick building, surrounded by trees and bushes, and it was here that the newspaper claimed Cosmogems ran its secret testing.

★   ★   ★

Cade's plane was delayed, and he finally stormed into the building just as most of the work force were leaving. Lexi was in her office when he flung open the door, the offending paper in his hand. He threw it on to her desk. 'Now will you believe there's a canker in the system? Only someone working for Cosmogems knows about this laboratory.'

'It's true then?' Lexi gasped in horror.

'Yes, we do have a lab in Scotland. It's high security because that's where we're doing work on skin cancers, and burns from radiation. Government work — top secret. Very few people know that.'

'But — animal experiments?'

A look of contemptuous scorn clouded Cade's face. 'What do you think? Of course it's not true. I'd never allow that. It's a tissue of scurrilous lies. I've already instructed my lawyers to deny and sue for libel. But we can't reveal the real nature of the work. Whatever we say, it's not going to ring true. Mud sticks, and there's already too much uncertainty about the future. Whoever started take-over rumours will have me to deal with. If you have anything to do with it, heaven help you. I'll make damn sure you never work in this country again — or anywhere where I have any influence.' He thrust the paper aggressively at her, his breathing ragged, his whole body tensed for the fight.

She stood up. 'Cade — please. I've no idea where that article came from. I didn't know anything about that lab — how could I? But I've something to tell you.' Lexi's office was small. Cade, his face storm force ten, leaned against her desk, his hands behind him. She came round to face him — there was little space between them. She drew a deep breath. 'You were right. There is someone — some people — who are working to harm Cosmogems. But I — you won't like what I have to say.'

He folded his arms and looked at her severely. 'Well?'

She paused. She didn't know how to begin. She'd rehearsed endlessly in her head, but now the words wouldn't come. She tried a devious route. 'Have you checked product costings lately?' She rushed on. 'There are adjustments made each month on our price lists — the ones that go out to customers are artificially inflated. Orders have dropped because prices seemed to be way above competitors' . . . I can't think how it was missed. That's what I found out in San Diego — there was a disk . . . '

'I know about that.' Cade spoke impatiently. 'I had a report from Mike Simmonds. Bella brought it on the plane. There's a bug in the computer system. A mistake apparently. I should have checked, but that's James' area. That's not sabotage, that's plain incompetence. It won't happen again. This,' he glared at the newspaper still on his desk, 'and all the stock exchange rumours are more serious. Is that all you have to tell me?'

Lexi couldn't believe it. How could he be so blind? She shook her head. 'It's not a bug, Cade. It's deliberate and, I'm afraid,' she swallowed, 'it's James and Bella who are at the bottom of it. And Mike Simmonds, too, your accountant.' The air froze. Cade was stone still. There was no sound from outside. Everyone had gone home, relieved not to have to face their boss at least until the morning. To Lexi, the silence lasted an eternity — so long, she had to speak. 'It's true. I'm sorry.'

Cade unfolded his arms, his whitened knuckles standing out from the tanned, clenced fists. 'I suppose you have evidence for your scandalous accusations.'

Lexi felt she'd been deposited in a desolate and unfriendly arctic wilderness. She'd no idea that a voice could sound so death chilled. Her own sounded high pitched, like a child's. 'I overheard them — Friday night — I was working late.'

'Ah!' His exclamation axed her sentence. 'So Bella was right. She told me you were snooping in my office when she and James were investigating the costings. She warned me you were out to make trouble.'

'Me make trouble!' She was incensed. 'I was working in your office because you told me you wanted me to use your computer, that's all. It's not true. Bella hinted at more trouble to come. James is going to take over from you.'

'James! That is ridiculous. James is my brother. Bella is my niece.'

'She hates you, Cade,' Lexi burst out, 'you've got to believe me.' But she knew he never would. Bella had dripped her poison in his ear on the New York trip. She'd had plenty of opportunity and, of course, he'd believed his family, rather than a comparative stranger. Lexi realised too, why Bella had buckled down and done such a magnificent job on Crystal Line. She appeared to be working to put the company back on the road, whereas, in fact, she was doing just the opposite. It was hopeless! She said dully, 'If you don't believe me, why don't you just let me go?'

His fists unclenched and, for a moment, Lexi thought he was going to hit her as he came menacingly closer. She tensed, ready to evade him, but he took her forearms in a strong grip, pulling her towards him. His eyes, topaz points of fury, bore into her, an angry pulse beat at his throat. He gave each word deliberate emphasis. 'No. Again. And again. It's no good trying to shift the blame in this ridiculous way. Sooner or later, you're going to make a mistake, and lead me to whoever is manipulating you. You are still my personal assistant. I can do exactly what I want with you — for six months. And you will never, ever, say another word against any member of my family.'

Lexi flung her head back, grey eyes flashing defiance, blonde hair tumbling over her shoulders. 'And if I leave anyway?'

His voice was gritty. 'But you won't, will you?' His lips were centimetres away from hers as he bent his head and kissed her with an authoritative force that sent her heart spinning. He held her in a crushing grip which melted her resistance. Her own lips parted in response as, with an inward grown of despair, she finally acknowledged that she'd fallen in love with her jailor. Almost as suddenly as he kissed her, he released her and stalked away . . . leaving her alone.

8

Every morning, in her head, Lexi vowed she would stay at home and look for another job. Yet, every morning her body automatically carried her to Cosmogems, ready to tackle anything he chose to throw at her. She justified what she considered to be her weak will, to Anya, by explaining how much she was sharpening up her business skills, ready for the future. Her friend, reasonably enough, pointed out that it was unlikely Lexi would ever have to launch a rescue operation for a company the size of Cosmogems.

Cade was superb. Swiftly he scotched all take-over rumours, with a statement that he was firmly in control of a viable company. He issued a libel writ against the newspaper which had published the offending article, and received a grudging apology, tucked away on an inside page.

But there were worrying factors which even Cade's confident authority couldn't override. In spite of the paper's backdown on animal experimentation, evidence of a laboratory working on something secret was irrefutable. The evasive explanation of what was going on there was unconvincing. The annual accounts were a final blow; due to be published within the next few days. For the first time in the firm's history, they would show a loss.

Cade had accepted the implausible explanation for the phoney costings. Lexi knew now that he had a totally blind spot about his family and would have — indeed had — accepted the flimsiest of explanations, rather than risk finding out the truth about his relatives. His main concern was to put Cosmogems back onto its feet. But the damage had been done. The company had had a consistently bad press, apart from Crystal Line, and even that initial impetus was slowing. Clients, customers, the general public — were fickle beasts. To them, Cosmogems was still suspect. Shares began to tumble again, and the battle moved into the Board Room.

A management faction called for a vote of censure on Cade, as the company Chairman. If it was carried, his resignation would be called for. An emergency meeting was called and, Lexi, by Cade's side in the Board Room, thought sadly how the working atmosphere had changed since her first meeting. Now, suspicions and mistrust clouded the air. Everybody knew that the company, maybe their jobs, were at risk. They waited for Cade to speak. She wondered how many of them had already made up their minds which way to vote.

In the Board Room setting, Cade looked magnificent; confident and powerful. One of life's winners! She didn't see how he could fail to carry his audience.

He began to speak quietly, the oldest trick in the book to command attention. 'I'd like to get this over as soon as possible. There isn't time to waste, agonising about what's gone wrong. Cosmogems is in crisis. There's a sickness at its heart which I should be able to cure. It seems I can't. There are forces at work — outside forces, bringing harm to our company.'

Lexi tried to keep her face expressionless. 'Outside forces'! This was Cade's weakness — an over-developed sense of family loyalty, getting the better of his business judgement.

His voice rose. 'I see little point in a vote of censure at this time. It will cause further confusions, uncertainties, which would lead to greater loss of confidence.' He paused, and looked across the table at James and Mike Simmonds. Both men refused to meet his eye. 'There has been financial mismanagement, absurd errors. I, ultimately, take responsibility for not keeping tighter control — for that you CAN censure me, but these errors won't be repeated, I guarantee that personally.'

There had been hostility in the room when Cade first came in, but Lexi could sense it evaporating as he spoke positively about the company's future, outlining plans for possible expansion in the States, developing new areas in the jewellery side. He spoke for an hour, ending with a pledge dedicating himself to Cosmogems. 'Not an ailing company,' he concluded, 'but one suffering a temporary virus which ultimately, will not do lasting harm.'

Lexi listened in despair. Bella was the main virus, with James and Mike very minor germs in comparison. Unless Cade could be made to see that, there was little hope for the company under his guidance. Bella would stop at nothing. Her contribution to the meeting was an outstanding example of Machiavellian practice. When the meeting was thrown open for discussion, James merely looked uneasy. Bella bided her time, until she saw the general trend swing to her uncle's favour. Then she spoke, employing a dangerous and devious strategy. She announced her support for Cade, and called for the resignation of Mike Simmonds, the Financial Director, and her fellow conspirator. Lexi could hardly believe her ears, and neither could Mike from the look on his face. He half rose to his feet, glared across at Bella, then slumped down again. He couldn't say a thing — she'd deny it, and he was still carrying the stain of the muddled costings. He would be implicated to the hilt. Serve him right, she thought acerbically, pretty sure that Bella's next move would be a ploy to get rid of her. Since the New York trip, Bella had been all sweetness and light to everyone except Lexi, for whom she reserved all her spite.

Cade brought the meeting to a close. 'There's no need for your resignation, Mike — for the moment.' The implication was ominously clear. A vote was taken. The censure motion was unanimously defeated. Cade thanked his staff formally, and left the meeting. 'Lexi, I want you in my office,' he called over his shoulder as he strode away.

'Doesn't he always?' Pete muttered, who'd been taking more than a passing interest in her lately, persistently asking her out. Lexi liked him, had been tempted, but he didn't stir her.

*   *   *

In the offices, the atmosphere was perceptibly more light-hearted. News had got around. Cade had survived, all would be well, and Christmas was only a few weeks away. It was much easier to believe that things would improve. Cade was popular with the work force, and he had their confidence. He'd done wonders in the past, so what were a few hitches? And look at Crystal Line. It was stocked in all the department stores, and of course, they gave Cade the credit for that. Thus ran the general tenor of the gossip and comment as people prepared to go home for the day, and strangely enough, as if the Stock Market itself had caught a whiff of the optimism, Cosmogems' shares ended the day's trading several notches up.

Only Lexi, it seemed, had lead in her heart. It couldn't work out. It was an impossible mess, and Cade's decree that she couldn't leave meant that she'd have to watch the whole disintegration proceed to its end.

Reluctantly, she went into his office. He was talking to a small, white haired man. The wall safe was open, and they were examining two identical sets of jewellery; necklace, bracelets, and ear-rings — both sets in velvet boxes. Jim Denton was the company expert in making replica jewellery — a growth area since the increased crime rate, and subsequent high insurance premiums.

He held out two jewel encrusted brooches to Lexi. 'Spot the false.'

She examined them closely. 'I can't. They both look expensive.'

Jim chuckled. 'Good girl — right answer. This one's worth thousands, and is destined for the bank vault. This one,' he held it up to the light, 'is Lady Lingard's Christmas present — to wear safely — at a fraction of the cost.'

Cade smiled at him indulgently. 'Well done, Jim. Now stop showing off and put those things back in the safe. Lexi and I have things to do.'

Not again, Lexi groaned to herself. She felt far too depressed to get her brain into the high gear Cade demanded. And when was she going to get her Christmas shopping done? 'It's nearly seven o'clock,' she said rebelliously.

Cade didn't reply for a moment, waiting until Jim had set the combination of the safe and left the office, bidding goodnight to both of them. 'Well, well, that's not like you, Lexi,' he drawled, completely relaxed in the big swivel chair, hands behind his head. 'I wasn't thinking of work on this occasion. I thought we might have supper together. Celebrate my reprieve this afternoon.'

'I don't think so, thank you.' She wasn't going to be caught again.

'Why not?' Cade's eyes glinted.

'Because . . . ' She stopped. A ready excuse didn't present itself. 'I don't want to,' she said abruptly.

He laughed aloud, and came to where she stood. He placed his hands on her shoulders, looking down into her face. 'You are lying, Lexi Brooke — deceiving yourself now. But not me — not this time! Get your coat! I know a good pub on the Brighton Road.'

'No — I'm . . . '

'Washing your hair? It really doesn't need it. You're coming with me, like it or not. Pretend it's work — you've still got six weeks to go. I see no reason for remission.'

* * *

Traffic was heavy getting out of London, and Cade drove in silence until it cleared, then he slipped a cassette into the sound system of the luxury limousine he'd chosen from the Cosmogems fleet to drive. 'Enjoy the perks while I'm still Chairman,' he'd said wryly when they purred away from the car park.

Soft, sensual music flooded the car's lush interior, and Lexi stiffened as Cade glanced towards her. 'Relax — you're very jumpy. There's nothing to be scared of, I haven't found you out — yet.'

'There's nothing to find out, not about me anyway,' she said, relishing the comfort of the soft leather upholstery, at the same time too aware of his long legs and hard thighs so close to her, the piquant tang of his body, the musky aftershave.

She'd bowed to the inevitable. It seemed that her much vaunted independence and strong will were myths, airy nothings, where Cade Chamberlayne was concerned. Otherwise, why was she now sitting opposite him in an, admittedly charming, country pub?

'Why have you brought me here?' She challenged him directly.

'Don't you like it? The food's good, and it's quiet — I thought it would be a nice change from the city.'

'You know precisely what I mean,' she said sharply. 'You've already given me the dinner treatment. Surely that was enough in the circumstances.'

'This is supper — more a pub meal.' His eyes were solemn, but there was a hint of mockery in their depths.

'Don't be so infuriating,' she snapped, slapping down the menu in frustration. There must be a reason, otherwise he'd be with his glamorous girlfriend.

'Come on, Lexi, it's a celebration — a double one.'

'Double?' Her attention was caught, as he'd known it would be.

'Surviving this afternoon — and an offer from San Diego.'

She looked at his mobile mouth, and the strong planes of his face. Everything about him spoke authority, but tonight there was something else — a supressed excitement, a wire taut expectancy that called to her own responses.

He studied the menu impatiently. 'Grilled salmon and Chablis?'

She nodded. Food was the last thing she wanted. 'What offer?' she prompted.

His voice betrayed his excitement. 'My own Research Centre in California, to study skin problems. Unlimited funding. Top scientists. Carte blanche!' He sat down, watching her carefully.

The colour drained from her face. 'But — Cade — you'd never leave Cosmogems. This afternoon — you promised.' He'd been so convincing, she felt a deep sense of disappointment — and loss. California?

'I'd said I'd had an offer, I didn't say I'd take it.' When, after a long pause, he said, 'I nearly got away once before.'

Lexi was astonished. 'But I thought you loved the job — the family company!'

Green and topaz merged into jewelled fusion as he smiled at her. 'I've told you several times, Miss Brooke, appearances can be deceptive. You, of all people, don't need me to tell you that.' She ignored the comment. 'I often envied brother Charles. He did his own thing — exploration. Pretended he was looking for gold mines. Really pulled the wool over Father's eyes. Spent years away, sending back the occasional telegram announcing, 'no luck so far', going on to whereever he fancied. Eventually, Father gave him up and concentrated on James and me. I'd just finished my science degree. I wanted to do research, but Father pushed me into a management course — he was a very forceful personality — some would say domineering.'

'I'd never have guessed.'

'You think I'm the same?'

'I didn't say so.'

'You didn't need to.'

She broke in. 'But why did you stay at Cosmogems. Couldn't James have taken over when your father and grandfather died? Left you to do research? You'd served your time.'

'Like Jabez for Maria?' He looked sceptical. 'There was a reason.'

'Tell me.'

Cade frowned, then lifted his hands in a 'what the heck' gesture. 'Oh well — it was a long time ago. I was very young and — besotted — with one of the Cosmogems models. It's messy. She blackmailed the company because of me. They supported me. I owe them support in return. And I can't leave now, not until Cosmogems is completely stable. Then — we'll see how things go.'

Lexi was silent. How ironical! If only Bella had waited, in the natural order of things, Cade would probably have relinquished control to James. Bella would soon have polished him off. And probably done a splendid job of running the company. She had flair and style, and was completely ruthless.

'Hey, don't look so sad, it wasn't that tragic — I survived.' He touched the corner of her eye in disbelief. 'Lexi! That's not a tear?'

'Certainly not.' She jerked away. 'It's the — er — the fish. I'm allergic to it.'

'Strange thing to order then.' His expression changed, his eyes roving over her heart shaped face, generous mouth, and honest grey-green eyes. Leaning towards her, he gently lifted her heavy hair and cupped her face in his hands. For a moment they looked into each other's eyes. 'Lexi, Lexi,' he murmured quietly, 'why did you walk into my office in that silly disguise? So like . . . ' He hesitated, searching her face, probing to the depths, then with a sigh, let her go. 'Never mind, it'll never happen again. I'll take you home.'

*   *   *

On the journey back there was no music. Cade said very little, his exhilaration had evaporated. The silence was uneasy, the air full of unspoken things, unfinished business. On the streets, garish fairy lights which had been up since November, swung pathetically in the wind and rain, reflecting Lexi's bleak mood.

As often happened, there was no parking space in the street near Anya's flat. Cade double parked, although there was a space further up. He leaned across to open the door, and she suddenly realised! It had been worrying her all evening. She swung round to face him. 'What a fool! Now I know why you told me — about San Diego. You . . . you devious . . . '

'What on earth?'

He sat back. A car behind flashed its lights — Cade's car was blocking the street. 'It's a test isn't it. You fed me that information deliberately. Oh, it'd make another good story, — 'Cade Chamberlayne drops Cosmogems for California', or in the tabloids — 'Rich Rat Leaves Sinking Hulk'! And it would be true. Of course, you'd deny you had any intention of leaving Cosmogems. You'd reaffirm your faith in the

Company. Sacrifice your big chance. Nothing wrong with the offer — just an interpretation of how you'd react. Just as only Bella and James would have known about the laboratory in Scotland — clever Bella only needed to hint at what might be going on there . . . '

'Lexi!' Cade's whiplash coincided with an impatient honking behind. She was half out of the car. 'Get back in. I'll park up there. We must talk.'

'No thanks, I've had it with you, Cade Chamberlayne. I see now why you asked me out to supper — and I nearly fell for it. You thought you'd finally catch me out. You've told no-one about your offer, have you? Just me! So,' now she was out on the street, anger and fury sparkled from her, 'if the story broke tomorrow, you'd know who it was. You actually thought it would be worth another upset, just to prove . . . ' Emotion took her words away. She slammed the car door with force, and saw Cade shoot out the other side. 'Don't come near me,' she yelled, running up the steps of Anya's building. 'I finally quit — so sue and be damned!'

'Lexi — stop.'

Cade was on the pavement when the driver of the car behind wound down his window. 'Are you going to move your car, Mate, or do I ram you out of the way. I don't care. My car's worth a fraction the value of yours.'

Cade's look was enough to scorch the vehicle to a frazzle but, with a last glare in Lexi's direction, he got back in and drove on. The empty spaces further up the street had been taken, and by the time he'd parked a couple of streets away and run back to Anya's flat, all the lights were out, and no-one answered his persistent ringing.

9

Lexi did go to work next day — to hand in her notice. Conditioning went deep, her integrity wouldn't allow her simply to walk out. She just prayed Cade wouldn't be there. Raised voices came from his office, the door was open, and Bella called out to her. 'You're here at last. Most of us have been at work for an hour or so.'

'Bella!' Madeleine's voice was shocked. 'Lexi's put in hundreds of hours of overtime. She doesn't have to clock punch.'

'She doesn't have to be here at all, as far as I'm concerned.' Bella's voice was spiteful.

As Lexi went into the office, the air smelt of disaster. Jim Denton looked miserable, Madeleine anxious, and Bella was Bella in her blackest mood. She noticed the door of the wall safe was open. Cade wasn't there.

Jim said, 'The jewels, you saw me put them in the safe?' Lexi nodded.

'They're gone. Only Cade, you, Madeleine, and I, have the combination. It's his personal safe. We usually keep the jewellery in a sealed vault. I brought the brooches up yesterday to show Mr Cade.'

'Well, he's probably got them,' Lexi said reassuringly.

'No. He'd leave a note — a trace — we always do that.'

Bella stepped forward. 'So — you have the combination, too. That was rather trusting of my uncle. I am surprised.'

Lexi went still. 'What are you implying?'

Bella laughed. 'Nothing, except that it would cause further distress to an already embarrassed company if it were to be known that Cosmogems couldn't even keep track of its customer's valuables.' Her voice was pure acid.

'Are you accusing me of taking

them?' Even Bella checked fractionally before the hauteur of Lexi's icy tone. Madelaine's hand flew to her mouth; Jim Denton looked wretched.

'No, but it would be very convenient for certain plans if those jewels were to be — well — mislaid for a while. Oh, I'm sure they'd turn up eventually, but by then the damage would have been done.'

Fury surged through Lexi. 'How dare you — you — accuse me. You know very well who's at the bottom of Cosmogems misfortunes — and I think it's about time everybody else knew too. Madeleine . . .'

'Stop it.' Bella moved swiftly and grasped Lexi's wrist, digging her long nails into the soft flesh. 'You — go now. AT ONCE! You've done enough damage to this company.'

'Don't be ridiculous.' Lexi tried to pull her hand away. 'Cade fires me — not you.' Bella tightened her grip, and pain shot through Lexi's arm.

A commanding voice broke into the

scene. 'What's going on? Bella, let go of Lexi. What do you think you're doing?'

'Cade — she's got to go. The Lingard jewels are missing, and she accused me . . . ' Bella's voice was hysterical. A fine act, thought Lexi cynically.

'Of course they're not missing. Lady Lingard's got them. I took them there this morning myself. What's been going on?' He was curt.

'You didn't leave a trace. We thought . . . ' Jim's voice was reproachful.

'Oh my goodness, I forgot. I didn't think anyone would go in the safe. I had to check on something. One of the clasps . . .

'Never mind now, Jim. The gems are safe.' He looked at the three women. 'This looks more serious. What happened?'

'She's got to go, Uncle Cade. Now!' Bella metaphorically stamped her foot, as Madeleine started to say something.

Lexi shook her head. 'It doesn't matter, I'm not staying. I told you last night. I'm quitting. I came to work out my notice, but it would be impossible to do that now.'

'You finish the six months,' Cade warned.

'Either she goes — or I do.' Bella's scowl marred her dark classic beauty.

'Well,' Lexi said quietly, 'there's no contest — there never would be. Madeleine, if you wouldn't mind sending on my things. It'll cause less embarrassment if I leave straight away.' She turned to Cade and held out her hand. 'And I'm truly sorry about the — deception. Oh — and you've seen the morning's papers? For once, not a mention of Cosmogems.'

Cade stood frowning. He ignored her hand, but his eyes, pure tiger topaz, looked deep into hers.

Lexi nodded to Jim and Madeleine, and walked out of the office. Her acting resources managed a normal smile in the outer office, even dredging up a joke about the increased amount of Christmas mail the staff was handling.

The cold air outside made her shiver. She'd left her jacket behind, but would rather die of pneumonia than go back for it.

Numbly, she drove out of the car park, through the security check out, producing her pass for the last time. The bar clanged down behind her. She drove a few hundred yards on — a left turn — and Cosmogems would be out of sight. She looked back, a last glance, and a terrified scream tore from her lips. A cracking roar coincided with a shooting sheet of flame, as glass splintered from a top window.

For a split second, there was complete silence, then alarm bells wailed, and people ran from the building. A dreadful pain squeezed the blood from her heart — Cade's office was behind that gaping hole, framed by jagged edged glass. The cream blinds flapped drunkenly down the walls in the chill December air. Lexi spun her car in a screaming turn, and sped back towards the barrier.

She had to wait for the evening to find out what had happened. The security guards had refused to let her back in — within minutes the police arrived and cordoned off the area. Lexi had to watch, shivering helplessly, while ambulances screeched in and out, blue lights flashing. Back at the flat, she'd tried to ring Cosmogems, but the lines were permanently engaged.

By six o'clock, a clear picture emerged. Lexi and Anya hung on to the newcaster's words: 'There was an explosion at Cosmogems gem and cosmetic's factory this morning, when an incendiary device, concealed in a letter bomb, exploded in Cade Chamberlayne's office. The letter had been addressed to the Chairman, marked 'Personal and Confidential'. The blast caused extensive damage to Mr Chamberlayne's office, and several of the staff were taken to hospital. Amongst the injured were the Chairman's secretary, and his niece, Mrs Bella Watson, a senior executive. We understand that no-one was seriously hurt, although Mr Chamberlayne has been transferred to a special burns unit. The extent of his injuries is unknown. There is an unconfirmed report that the bomb was the work of a group called 'Activists for Animal Freedom'. This is the latest trouble to hit Cosmogems . . . ' Anya moved quickly and turned off the set.

'Burns!' Lexi sprang up in horror. 'I've got to see him.'

'Ring the hospital first. His family will be there.'

'Ugh! James — Bella — some family! How could they . . . ?'

'We don't know yet,' Anya pointed out. 'I'll ring the burns unit. You're shaking.' She found the number and dialled. Lexi, tense at her side, waited in agony until she'd put the phone down and smiled. 'He's OK. Honestly. They're not sure yet about the degree of burns. Only close family are allowed to visit. It'll be a couple of days before they know how damaged his hands are. You'll just have to be patient.

As the days passed with agonising slowness, Lexi changed her mind. After the first shock, she realised it would be futile to see Cade again. It was clear what he thought of her, and to see him would revive all her longings. She would go abroad. Listlessly, she began a job search, prepared to accept anything half-way suitable. She put out several feelers for jobs in Europe and, when the phone rang one afternoon, she picked it up expecting to hear news of a possible interview.

'Lexi, it's Madeleine. Why haven't you been in touch?'

'Madeleine. I'm sorry. It was difficult. How are you . . . and Cade?'

'I'm fine, and he's not too bad. Lexi . . . ' there was a pause, 'I don't know how you feel about this — but — Cade's told me to give you a message. He says, and I quote exactly, 'For God's sake, Maddy, if you don't get Lexi here at once, I'll get out of this damned bed and fetch her myself'.'

'Oh, Maddy, why does he want to see me?'

'I can't imagine,' his secretary replied drily, 'but you know Cade. 'At once' means 'at once'. I should go now. He's got a private room — there're no restrictions.'

'Bella? James?'

'He'll tell you. Don't worry, they won't be there. Good luck — and Lexi — see you soon.'

She took her car — a taxi would have been too slow — and left it in a spot where it was practically guaranteed to be clamped. She didn't care. A nurse showed her the way, and she ran down the corridor, then stopped at the door, suddenly uncertain.

'Lexi — don't stand there — come in.' The deep familiar voice — unchanged, commanding.

She went closer and caught a breath. 'Cade, you look — exactly the same!' she burst out in relief. Apart from blistering and a roughened texture, his face looked normal. 'Your hands!'

'Better than they look.' He lifted two white ointment smeared polythene bags. 'Come here,' he said gruffly, 'where I can get at you.'

She went to him, and found herself folded in his arms. His mouth sought hers, and she yielded with a sigh. The kiss was gentle, but the promise of passion blazed in the brilliant eyes, as his lips reluctantly left hers.

'Miss Brooke,' he said hoarsely, 'you have me at a distinct disadvantage. Just you wait until I get out of here.'

'Cade — what about Cosmogems?'

'I owe you an apology. You were right. After the bomb, James was so scared, he told me the whole sorry story. It's a mess, but nothing I can't deal with, now it's in the open.'

'They didn't send the bomb?'

'No. Some crazy group who obviously didn't believe we weren't animal testing. Bella and James are two very shaken people and, don't forget, Bella was in the office when the bomb exploded.'

'Where is she now?'

'Abroad. A long holiday. If she can sort herself out, I may let her loose on New York — heaven help them. James is much chastened. He'd like a second chance, and it'd be useful to keep him at Cosmogems if I want to take the Californian option. He was very much under Bella's influence, and I think even she didn't realise how things would snowball. She was mad at me to begin with, then it became a game she had to win! But it's over now, and I can put Cosmogems right.'

'After that, you're going to California?' Lexi was surprised that she kept the quaver out of her voice.

'That depends on you.' He gave her a look that constricted her throat, then he said, 'Whether you marry me.'

'Marry you — but . . . '

Her senses sang to a wild rhythm as Cade pulled her down onto the bed and kissed her again. 'No buts,' he commanded. 'I love you, Lexi. I've fought it far too long. I can't look at you any longer without wanting you, wanting to be with you, for ever.'

Cade loved her! She thought of all the wasted days. 'Why did you have to fight it, Cade?'

'Because, when you walked into my office as Miss Efficient, I knew that there was something . . . but I denied it — because — it happened once before.' Lexi's grey eyes were puzzled and he kissed her again for a long time. 'You will marry me — soon?' His breath was ragged.

'You know I love you, Cade. Of course I will. But,' even through her sun-bursting happiness, curiosity piqued, 'what happened?'

'Before?' Cade sighed. 'OK, then we'll concentrate on us. The past's a foreign country now. I don't want to visit it. You're not in it, my darling love.' He spoke rapidly, as though ridding himself of a burden. 'The girl, the one I told you about, the one who black-mailed the family — she first applied for a job with Cosmogems — as my father's secretary. At the interview, she was dressed not unlike you — neat, prim, efficient. As soon as she was established — WHAM — out came the glamour. She'd tried for modelling before, and been turned down. This was her way in, and she was totally unscrupulous. I was incredibly naive and, when it was all over, it hurt. That's why, when you appeared — allied to all Cosmogems problems ... I didn't recognise your honesty, your sweet integrity. I've been a blind fool, but I'm going to make up for it. And now, for God's sake, let's stop talking. I'm getting out of here, whatever the doctors say. We'll get married at Christmas.' Lexi gasped.

'That's next week!! I'm going home to see my family.'

'That's fine, we'll have them at the wedding. I'll arrange a special licence — but then — I want you to myself. A very long honeymoon. I know just where I'm taking you.'

'Where?' Lexi could hardly breathe

for the happiness exploding through her.

Before he finally stopped the talking with a deeply passionate kiss, Cade said, 'To Mexico, of course. To show you the gems of the desert. There's to be no more deception — ever!'

As his lips descended on hers Lexi, winding her arms round his neck, had time to murmur, 'There'll never be any need — ever.'

THE END